Frankie Zapper

and the

Disappearing Teacher

CHILDREN'S BOOKS
BY LINDA ROGERS

Worm Sandwich

Brown Bag Blues

The Magic Flute

Kestrel and Leonardo
(with Susan Musgrave)

Frankie Zapper

and the

Disappearing Teacher

by

LINDA ROGERS

Drawings by

RICK VAN KRUGEL

RONSDALE/CACANADADADA

RONSDALE PRESS
A Cacanadadada Production
3350 West 21st Avenue
Vancouver, B.C. Canada
V6S 1G7

Set in Sabon 13 on 16
Typesetting: The Typeworks, Vancouver, B.C.
Printing: Hignell Printing, Winnipeg, Manitoba
Cover Art: Rick Van Krugel
Cover Design: Cecilia Jang

The publisher wishes to thank the Canada Council and the British Columbia Cultural Services Branch for their financial assistance.

CANADIAN CATALOGUING IN PUBLICATION DATA

Rogers, Linda, 1944–
Frankie Zapper and the disappearing teacher

ISBN 0-921870-27-2

I. Van Krugel, Rick, 1947– II. Title.
PS8585.O392F7 1994 jC813′.54 C94-910391-8
PZ7.R633Fr 1994

This book is for
Tristan, Jenny, and Harry
and in memory of
Sam Page and Brad van Krugel
with thanks to
the hospitable Cowichan people, especially
Leonard Peter, the Gibson family,
and Maggie and Vernon (Sassy) Jack.

1

Odie Gets an Idea

"Frankie Zapper can change the channels without touching nothing." SuperJen was jumping up and down, causing the six-guns printed on her wild-west socks to just about shake out of their holsters. She was making such a commotion, Odie was sure windows were cracking a mile away.

"Settle down, Jen. You're breaking the sound barrier."

"Odie, listen to me. I saw it with my own eyes. Frankie wished and it happened. He changed the channels with magic. Do you understand what I'm saying?"

"So?" Odie gave her his famous exasperated eyeballs rolled back right over the rims of his glasses and into the back of his head look.

"Odie, do I have to spell it out for you? F-R-A-N-K-I-E Z-A-P-P-E-R C-A-N..."

"Shut-up, Jen, and pass me the copper sulphate." Odie was busy with his new science kit, which had come with the wrong set of instructions. He was already frustrated, and Jen was getting on his nerves.

Her enthusiasms usually lasted about as long as a jawbreaker. One day she was bouncing holes in the roof, and the next she couldn't remember what it was that had got her so excited in the first place.

If he could just get her off the subject of Frankie, maybe she would forget, and Frankie's secret would be safe between the two boys. Jen just couldn't be trusted with that kind of information. She had the biggest mouth in grade six, maybe even the entire school.

She squinched her eyes, found the right bottle, passed it to him and watched him mix it with vinegar. "Oo, what's that?" She plugged her nose. It smelled awful.

"An artificial fart," Odie laughed, pleased with himself.

"You're gross." She jerked her arm back and collided with a jar full of something red and nasty which spilled and actually began to eat up the table. Odie watched its terrible progress with horror. If that stuff landed on his new white carpet, he was a goner.

"Jen! What a klutz! She's gonna kill me!" Odie's mother was out at the gym. Since she had started lifting weights, she had become so strong Odie and his dad were both terrified of her. A simple hug was enough to make their hair stand on end. Just that week she had carried a sofa all the way up from the basement by herself.

Jen was using her shirt to clean up the mess."I'm sorry. I'm sorry." When she got upset, she talked like a typewriter.

He was starting to feel sorry for her. "Look what you're doing to your shirt." The chemical was making little holes where she'd used it to mop up. "It looks like grandpa's sweater after my hamster ate it."

"Quit changing the subject, Odie. You tell me about Frankie or I'm going to tell all the kids at school that your real name is Ormonde Dupuys, after your grandfather."

"One thing I just hate about you, Jen. You

fight dirty." There were tears in his eyes, and he knew she had him. What was the point in being friends, anyway, if you didn't share everything?

"I know you know about Frankie, and I never kept a secret from you in my life."

"That's not true. What about the cake you won at the school fair?"

"I told you about that."

"Sure. After you ate it."

"Well, you and Frankie were smoking comics behind the gym. I couldn't find you."

"You could've waited."

"It was an ice cream cake, and it was melting. Besides, you had a stomach-ache. You threw up. I remember what you said after. You said you rushed to the toilet but the throw-up ran faster than you did." He laughed.

It was true. Smoking the rolled-up funny papers was Frankie's idea. He saw it in Mad Magazine.

"Come on, Odie. Hurry up." Jen had hold of his wrist and she was moving it slowly up his back.

"Okay. Okay. Let me go." She released his arm. "I know all about Frankie. I've known it for ages. He must be a wizard or something. I've seen him do stuff like that and I've looked it up in the library. I think it has something to do with being an Indian. You can catch it from a dead relative. His grandfather was a medicine man, and he made people who were sick or crazy get better with magic."

"Like Jesus," Jen said. The year her mother got saved by the guy on T.V., she had to go to Sunday school. It was O.K., except that she had to wear a dress. She hated the lessons, but she liked the singing and the pictures and the kool-aid and cookies.

"I guess so." Odie's parents slept in on Sunday, and he'd never been inside a church. "Anyway, you can't go around blabbing about this. Frankie would get awful mad. He doesn't want people turning him into a freak and using him to get their homework done. He doesn't even use magic to do his own. I can't figure that part out. How come Frankie is so smart in some ways and not in others? If he can do spells, why can't he do math?"

"Well, look at you." Jen's nose twitched. She was dying to pick it, but she knew Odie would notice and maybe he'd tell since she had started things by threatening him. "You can't spell and you're a genius. You can do math and experiments and tricks with coins and the little sticks with diamonds in them."

"Rhinestones, Jen." He was trying to find the words that would make her understand the difference. "I can do tricks, but not real magic. Not like Frankie. He's special." Odie was getting carried away with praise. He raised his arms in the air and just about knocked Jenny's nose off her face. It was her fault for standing so close to him he could smell her supper. "Frankie Zapper is a real true genius."

"Gee, you're lucky he didn't put a hex on you that time you put that pellet in his cheek and he had to have three stitches. He could've had the ghoulies come in the night and suck your blood."

"I know." Odie and Jen were whispering and their foreheads were just about touching. They could hear the sound of the garage door being slammed shut by a muscular woman. In a minute, his mother would be sneaking up on them with a list of chores or the mangled remains of a bicycle left in the driveway. "I never told you but Frankie is the one who broke Nelson Baine's arm."

"How'd he do that?"

"Remember the time Nelson called Frankie Francis and told all the kids his mother cut his hair?"

"Yeah?"

"Well, right after that, Nelson fell down the stairs and ccchhhk," Odie made a noise with his teeth that sounded exactly like a bone breaking.

"Psychedelic, blows the mind out of proportionate thinking. It could have happened to you. Both arms. Fingers, everything. You'd have to quit playing the piano."

Odie grinned, showing all his fur-covered teeth. What a beautiful thought. No more practising. No more terrible recitals, all those girls in pink net dresses and Odie the only male for miles around, his body forced into a three-piece junior executive suit Wonder Woman bought on sale at K-Mart.

"Jen, it wasn't my fault about the gun. We were trying to hide it on his brother because he wanted to shoot squirrels. It went off when we were hiding under the bed. Frankie wasn't mad at me. It was an accident. Besides, he got presents and all the grown-ups and kids felt sorry for him. It was the best time he ever had in his life."

"You could have been arrested."

"Jeez Jen, I felt sick. I was scared to death. I though he was going to die and they'd cancel Christmas or something."

"Boy, I wish they had. I wish they'd called off the school concert. I hated having to be Santa with a plasticene nose and three pillows, just because Frankie Zapper was lying on his bed of pain reading comics and eating ice cream."

"Mr. Smith said we did the worst Christmas play he ever saw in his life."

"He always says that. My sister told me he thinks every class is the worst class he ever had."

"Mr. Smith is the worst teacher I ever had." Odie was making himself miserable. He had lost interest in his experiments.

"I hate Mr. Smith."

"He has horrible breath."

"Somebody told me he eats snakes."

"I heard he used to eat kids in the old days before they stopped him. He wasn't allowed to give detentions anymore, because a lot of kids disappeared after school."

Jen was trying to remember all the awful things. "Have you noticed how he gets those big wet marks under his arms everytime a parent comes for a conference? I just love it when that happens. He looks scared to death."

"I wish he'd die."

"I don't know, Odie. I just want him to go away and do another job. He's got a daughter and she's perfectly normal. I saw her with him at a garage sale. She might miss him if he died." Jen missed her dad and he was only divorced, not dead at all.

Odie was putting his tubes and chemicals away in the box that came with the wrong instructions. "I doubt that she loves him. I'll bet he tortures her. Probably he makes her do math on Saturdays, when we're all at the movies throwing popcorn over the balcony and putting sucked candies on the seats, so they'll stick to people."

"I still don't think you should have said that. What if Frankie heard you? He can make wishes come true. If he can change the channel and make Nelson Baines fall down the stairs, he could kill Mr. Smith. We'd be criminals, excessives."

"Accessories, Jen."

"We'd be accessories and they'd send us to the electric chair." She sure knew how to make her eyes wide.

"Jen, you've given me a wonderful idea. If I was six inches taller, I'd kiss you."

2

Odie and Frankie Get Down to Business

Frankie Zapper's mum was sitting in front of the television set with her knitting, turning a big ball of grey wool into a sleeve. On the floor beside her was the back of a sweater with the black and white eagle design and several Double Bubble wrappers. As she knitted, Mrs. Zapper blew bubbles as big as her face and then carefully swallowed them back.

"It's real good exercise for your chin," she said, offering some to Odie and Jen, who was marvelling at the way the needles moved as fast as the speed of light in her fingers. "You'll find out when you get to be my age." Jen didn't think so. Everybody said she was skinny because she was so hyperactive. She couldn't imagine ever sitting still long enough to make her chin fat and wobbly.

"I had a wool sweater once," Jen said, picking up a handful and watching light come through the lovely creamy stuff that hadn't been spun yet, "but my mum shrank it. It got all hard and it fitted my doll. Now I have to wear, whatdoyoucallems, symplicits—those things you can put in the washing machine—because my grandma says she won't knit me one more thing, if my mum's going to wreck them.

"I liked that sweater," she said with a big sigh. "It had real pearl buttons on it."

It was magic watching little knots of wool transform into something somebody was going to wear. Mrs. Zapper walked through her whole day with knitting in her hands, chewing gum, cooking, watching T.V., and minding her kids, and she never dropped a stitch. Whenever Jen tried to do two things at once, like babysitting and talking to her friends, it always ended in a disaster.

Just last week, the Mulholland baby got into five pounds of liquid honey, while Odie was telling Jen how to do her math homework over the phone. It took her three hours to clean up the mess, and Mrs. Mulholland didn't pay Jen, because she said it was her fault and honey was expensive.

At this moment, Odie was pacing back and forth in front of the T.V., causing Mrs. Zapper's favourite soap opera to flicker in the most irritating way. He was tired of waiting for Jen to finish her visiting, and Mrs. Zapper was cracking her gum, because she was tired of having him block her vision.

"Come on, Jen." He jumped over the pile of

carded wool and grabbed Jen's hand before he remembered. Now he was in for it. A fuse blew in his brain when he realised what he had done. He had been so careful not to touch her fingers since all the little warts appeared the summer of the tadpole hunts. He cursed himself for his stupidity, but he didn't want to let go now and hurt her feelings. She'd probably start to cry or something in front of Frankie's mum, and then he would feel like a goof.

Holding Jen's hand felt about as pleasant as eating liver. Plug your nose and eat, he said to himself. Maybe it wouldn't happen. Maybe they'd stay put instead of sliding over onto his fingers. He hoped so. Warts were about as gross as you could get, worse than getting pin-worms because everybody could see them.

"See ya, Miz Zapper." They disappeared into the room Frankie shared with his sisters. Zapper wasn't their real name. Everybody called Frankie "Zapper", because of the spitballs.

He collected the silver stuff in cigarette boxes, made little cups out of the foil, chewed the paper part until it was gooey, put the paper in the cups and threw them against the wall, and they stuck. The name stuck too.

The only one in the class who knew or cared about Frankie's real last name was Mr. Smith. He also called him Francis.

Mr. Smith stuck to every rule. It was like his

body was covered with crazy glue and little paper "thou-shalt-nots", like the loony downtown who walked around pushing a grocery cart with prayers and pages from the Bible attached to it with clothes-pins. Their teacher never smiled when somebody cracked a funny or broke wind, and he refused to call Frankie "Zapper", because it wasn't on his birth certificate.

Frankie was lying on his bed, one leg crossed over the other, hands folded behind his head, admiring the collection on his ceiling. The roof of his room looked like a cave full of stalactites. This was the way he tripped at home, cutting out all the noise, concentrating on the twinkling zaps and letting his mind go free.

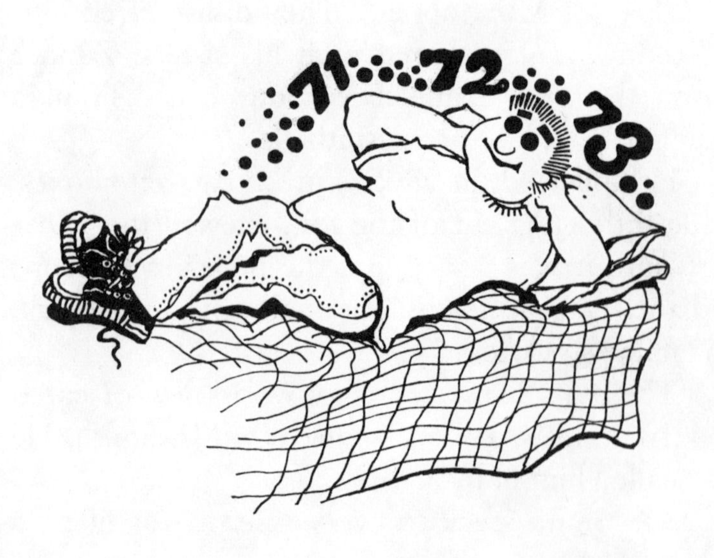

At school it was different. He stared out the window and dreamed of being a kite or a bunch of helium balloons flying off into the clouds with their strings dangling.

It made Mr. Smith furious when Frankie took off on his daydreams. He even tried shutting the curtains, but Zapper could see through cloth. He could dream his way through metal. When they talked about the Iron Curtain in Social Studies, Odie looked at Frankie, glassy-eyed and lost in his thoughts, and he knew he could cut through anything, like a diamond drill or a singer with a high squeaky voice.

Odie had known about his friend's special vision for ages. He noticed stuff like that, every little detail. A relentless investigator, he knew who wet their beds, who sucked their thumbs, and who stole candy from the Tuck Shop down the street from the school.

Sometimes Frankie and Odie worked together. The year before, when Odie was class president, somebody was stealing the desserts from people's lunch-boxes. It turned out to be Charlotte. She never knew how she got caught, but it was Frankie who solved the crime. He just turned his eyes on her bulging tummy and described its contents to Odie, who had taken inventory of cookies and cake and candy bars in the cloak-room first thing in the morning, while everyone else was at assembly.

Later, they got Charlotte behind the swings and told her they'd cut off her braids and use them for brooms if she ever did it again. That was the end of the lunch raids.

For a long time, the magic was their secret. They didn't talk about it much. Odie noticed things happening and Frankie knew. They didn't want Jen to find out, because she had so much trouble keeping secrets. In a way, it was unfair, but it was for everybody's good. The day he changed the channels just by wishing and wiggling his ears, he had forgotten she was there, quiet for a change and concentrating on his mother's knitting.

"Hi Jen. Hi Odie." Frankie wasn't too enthusiastic. He was counting his zaps. There were seventy-three from one corner diagonally to another in the room he shared with his three sisters, the youngest of whom was reading a 3-D Three Stooges comic in her bed at that very moment.

Seventy-three was space travel, one of Frankie's favourites. Jen and Odie were interrupting. Worse, he could tell they were on a serious mission and he didn't want Little Big Ears in the corner to hear. There was no end to what might happen if she found out he could pull ice cream cones out of his pockets or change the marks on her report card.

"What's up?" He rolled over and fixed his brown eyes on Odie's winking glasses, which were directly in the path of the sunlight that directed his magic trips across the ceiling.

"We gotta talk." Odie jerked his finger in the direction of the Little Sister Who Listened and Told.

"Ya Frankie, Odie has an idea."

"Oh, oh," the young magician rolled out of bed, revealing quite a few Tootsie Roll wrappers and Jen noticed with disappointment none of them were fat and promising, full of candy.

"Got any more?" she tried anyway. Her appetite knew no limits.

"Nope." Frankie was shoving his feet into a pair of black basketball runners, held together with safety pins. They were his favourites. He was trying to stop his feet from growing, so he could wear them forever. His sisters said they smelled, but he

didn't care. He loved those shoes. "I'm awful tired," he said, hoping they'd decide to go away at the last minute. His mind got worn out counting and wishing for trips.

"It's about Mr. Smith," Odie gave what his musclebound parent called his up-to-no-good diabolical smile.

Frankie's stomach flopped over. Mr. Smith had just been to see his mother about the afternoon he missed when he decided to take himself on a field trip to Goldstream River to see the fish spawn. Stars and fish were his favourite things. That and zaps. They had so much light, he could watch them forever.

His stolen afternoon had been wonderful, worth the trouble he was going to get into. He felt his heart beat in his ears as he biked along the highway to the river, moving softly between two walls of fern-covered rock. There was a clear autumn sun and he felt dizzy with the colours of the leaves dying on the trees and fish changing colour too, as they struggled to the place of their birth to lay eggs and die.

There were other Indians there with spears and jigging hooks and lines. They waited patiently, protecting their eyes from the river's glare with polaroid glasses. The fish and the men and boys all knew each other. Their kinship was knowing sooner or later they would all be somebody's dinner, food on a plate or compost for graveyards, pushing up daisies or wild asparagus.

The question was, who would win this time? The excitement of it was something they could almost hold in their hands and feel.

Frankie didn't care so much about that part. He didn't enjoy the actual fishing. What he loved was the flash of silver sides in water, the bubble and splash. He stood as still as a tree all afternoon, watching and listening.

When Mr. Smith came to report that Frankie played hookey, he freaked out, threatening Frankie's mum with words like truancy and welfare workers. Frankie was tempted to ask her knitting needles to fly out of her hand and attack Mr. Smith.

"Fish," he said to himself. It was a word full of power and magic.

"Frankie, quit daydreaming." Jen couldn't wait another second to move out of there and get on with her business.

As they trudged through the living room, Mrs. Zapper looked up and smiled. She didn't ask her son where he was going and when he was coming back. He was like the wind. He never turned up when he said he would anyway, and she knew that. Wherever he was, he would make sure he was fed on time. Frankie had the look of a human garbage can that was an inspiration to mothers. They couldn't wait to stuff him, and, when he ate, he made little mm good noises that drove them wild. As far as they were concerned, Zapper was a prince among boys and his manners were perfect.

"My stomach's aching," he said when they were outside. "Let's go down to the Cedar Cafe and have some chips and gravy." Frankie had picked up the gravy habit from Odie, who started having it on french fries to discourage his always-dieting parents from stealing them off his plate after they ordered only salad for themselves in restaurants.

Odie paid. He'd just received his allowance and he wanted his friend in a good mood.

The kids all loved the Cedar. The chips there were big and fat and they gave huge servings and never complained about how much ketchup got used up. Also, there was a juke box that was broken and they could get as many songs as they liked for a quarter. Hardly any grown-ups went there to wreck their fun, at least not parents. The place was like a club. Joe, the owner, was a big brother to all the kids. He knew about everybody's home run, whose parents were getting divorced and who was in the Black Book at school.

"Frankie," Odie said finally, when the last gravy-soaked chip disappeared. "I can't stand another minute of Mr. Smith. Two years with one teacher is criminal. We've got one thousand and twenty hours left." A big tear rolled down his cheek.

"Do you know how many minutes that is?" He stood up, knocking over the ketchup. "I'm going to have a nervous breakdown. I can't sleep at night. I can't keep anything down except Kraft Dinner and Oreos." He swept his sleeve through the spilt ketchup. "I can't concentrate on my experiments. You've got to make him disappear."

"Sit down Odie," Frankie said, licking his fingers. "I'll try."

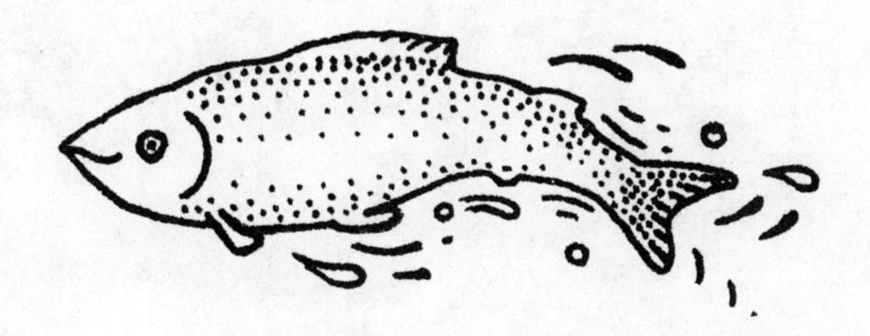

3

At the Graveyard

The three friends were sitting on the damp ground covering the grave of Frankie's late uncle, while they waited for Jenny's warts to disappear. Graveyard magic was supposed to work on warts, but it was getting later and later and still nothing had happened. They were all very depressed.

"How did he die?" Odie asked, trying to forget his shivers and concentrate on the dead body underneath them. He wished he'd worn all his sweaters. He wished he hadn't come at all. The thought of his cosy, warm bed was almost more than he could stand.

"His brother shot him." Frankie told them in his most solemn and pitiful voice. "It was an accident. He thought he was a deer."

"Ho-ly!" Jen screeched and Odie wanted to sew her lips with skipping rope. "Just like you and Odie. Gee, you could have been dead too, Frankie."

"Yeah, and you could have had the day off school to go to my funeral." He was enjoying the picture. Everyone would cry if he died and say what a good guy he was. They would be sorry, especially his mother and father. They would wish they never spanked him and would regret never giving him a brand new bike. His mother and sisters would make pies and cakes and his dad would catch a ton of fish and smoke it for the wake.

"It was only a .22," Odie said, peevishly. "I only got him in the cheek."

"Where'd he get it, Frankie?"

"Who?" Frankie's mind was off and running elsewhere.

"Your uncle, stupid."

"Right through the heart," he guessed. Actually, he had no idea. It had happened a long time ago, before he was born. His uncle was just a boy like him. He and his brother were out shooting deer for their naming dance.

His uncle's name was going to be First Bird of Summer, like the cousin who owned a song that sounded like "the salmon berries are ripe". Frankie's mum told him all this. She didn't like her kids having guns, but his dad insisted. A man had to know how to get his own food.

It really didn't help, knowing the sad story of Joe Thomas, who died violently at the age of twelve, exactly their age. They felt creepy sitting near all those tombstones and crosses, hearing his dead bones rattle under the ground.

"I hear moaning and dead bones," Jen said.

"No, you don't," Odie said sharply. "It's wind and the leaves. Stop being a jerk."

"I'm not a jerk."

"Well then, you're a turkey."

"I'm not a turkey either."

"So stop acting like one."

"I am not. Look who's talking. You didn't even get born. You were the booby prize in a lottery."

"That's not true, Jenny," he answered haughtily. "My parents never buy raffle tickets. They don't believe in it."

"It's no good." Frankie was fed up. It was all his fault. He should never have let them talk him into this. He couldn't get rid of warts and he couldn't get rid of Mr. Smith. It was useless to try. He felt cold and miserable and his nose was running. He wanted to wipe it with his sleeve but a voice that sounded strangely like his mother's was whispering in his ear. "Knock it off, son. Use a kleenex. I didn't go to all that trouble to knit you something to blow your nose on."

"But I don't have a kleenex." He thought out loud.

"What did you say?" Jen asked.

"It's just his voices." Odie was telling her to shut-up and let Frankie think. If this part of the plan didn't go properly, then all would be lost.

Frankie was getting more and more depressed. "How am I going to make Mr. Smith disappear if I can't even do it to Jen's warts? You've got to face it. I'm a failure."

Jenny and Odie were stamping their feet, trying to get warm. They were scared of the dark and scared of getting caught in the Indian cemetery, in the middle of the night, with their pyjama legs rolled up under their coats. Jen was worried somebody might see the chair she left outside her bedroom window and tell.

Her mother would go crazy if she turned on the lights and saw the red head on Jen's pillow was just a floor mop. Probably it would be in the newspaper too. There would be a story about her warts on the

front page. The whole town would be talking about her. When she grew up, no one would marry her.

"Maybe we remember it wrong. I never read the book and they might have left something out in the movie."

"I read the book," Odie said. "It's my fault. I should have insisted on the dead cat. There are always lots of them on the highway." His throat kind of squeezed itself when he thought of all the furry wrecks that didn't get to finish crossing the road. "I could have picked one up, I think. I'm not afraid of blood and guts."

"Stop it, Odie. I don't want any dead cats. I'd rather have warts." Now she was crying because all this horrible talk made her remember the time her kitten got shut in the dryer.

It happened the very same week her dad left. Her parents had a terrible fight, and he went away without saying good-bye or even taking his beer out of the fridge. After he left, her mum never stopped crying, and, for a long time, Jenny had to do all the housework and cooking and everything.

Her kitten must have been looking for a warm place to sleep. Jen thought maybe she had a bad dream and walked in her sleep. She could have turned the dryer on. In the morning, the cat was dead and there was dried blood all over the sheets and towels. "No cats! That's for ordinary people. Frankie has magic and he doesn't need all that stuff for a spell."

"I can't do it," Frankie wailed. He sure could have used a Mars Bar to perk up his blood sugar and make him feel better. He got crabby when he was hungry. Odie would have got him something sweet if it was humanly possible in a graveyard at three in the morning. "I can't make it happen if it doesn't want to."

Jen and Frankie were losing their nerve. Odie had to get the situation back under control. They were on a secret mission against the forces of darkness and everything depended on him staying cool. "Listen," he said. "There could be a lot of reasons why they won't go away. We did everything else right. We tied three knots in a string and touched your warts with raw meat and you buried it in a secret place."

"But you know where it is."

"I didn't look, Jen. Honest. And neither did Frankie. I think you don't want them to disappear badly enough."

"I do!" Jen practically yelled. "They're ugly."

Odie and Frankie didn't say anything nice, like "No, they're not," because that would have been a lie. Warts were gross. Warts looked terrible and they felt terrible and they were probably catching. They all knew about Tom Sawyer and Huck Finn and they knew the spells they did to get rid of the disgusting bumps were true. They had to be.

"Maybe it's the spirit of your dead uncle," Odie volunteered after some thought. "Maybe he's playing tricks on us. It must be boring lying in a coffin all the time. The only people who ever come here are old fogies visiting their dead relatives and the guys who dig the holes and cut the grass. I bet he hardly ever sees kids like us."

"That's it!" Frankie jumped up and grabbed Odie's arms like he was going to shake him or hug him. "He's fooling around with our spell!"

"Of course," Jen agreed. She didn't want to take the blame for it not working, after all the trouble they'd been to. They'd never let her forget that her warts were stubborn or that she wasn't suggestible.

Odie told her you had to be smart to be suggestible. Dumb people didn't get the right vibrations.

It was hard being around a brain like Odie all

the time. It made her feel stupid. "I'll bet he's real lonesome. Maybe we should talk to him."

"Don't be dumb, Jen." He must have been reading her thoughts. As far as he was concerned, her mouth got her in enough trouble without messing around with ghosts, who were known to be temperamental and cause all kinds of trouble. He had read stories about people who had to leave their houses because the ghosts that lived there didn't like them. They were all freaked out by that

movie where the creepies came out of their graves and wrecked a housing development, because it was built on the place where they were sleeping. It made their hair hurt when the ghosts and ghoulies came out of cupboards and swimming pools and grabbed people by the ankles and wrists or turned meat into maggots. Odie felt sick to his stomach.

"What worries me," Frankie explained, getting them back to the subject of Mr. Smith, "is this. I'm afraid I might wreck it somehow. What if he half-disappeared and his feet started running around the school kicking everybody because he was mad?

"What if I couldn't get rid of his top half and we still had to look at his icky face? If that happened, he could tell on us and we'd all go to jail forever and ever. It would be worse than getting killed." Frankie looked at his uncle's tombstone, and made a tragic face.

Jen agreed. "Even if it was just his voice and the rest of him was invisible. He could still make trouble." Mr. Smith was an awful tattle tale. Just last week he told her mother about the time she wore lipstick to school, because he knew she wasn't allowed to have it. What a pig. Her mother made her wash the basement floor with a toothbrush and it was all his fault.

"I don't care," Odie said. "You're acting like wimps. I think Frankie should try anyway. Things can't be any worse than they are now. It's not as though we're going to KILL Mr. Smith. We're just vanishing him. I'll bet Frankie can bring him back when we finish grade six. He could just make him into something else for a while. Something nice, like a flower or an animal."

"Nothing you can eat." Jenny said.

"Oh, puke." Odie answered.

"I don't know, Odie. I think that's selfish. If we just vanish him for this year, what'll happen to the next class? He'll be ten times meaner afterward." Frankie was actually thinking of his little sister. Even though she had big ears and a blabbermouth, he was fond of her. After all, she was his own flesh and blood.

"Listen," Odie told them. "We can work out the details later. I think we should go home and sleep on it. I have a feeling that when Jen wakes up tomorrow, her warts will all be gone. Everything will be fine in the morning and we can figure it out from there."

He was right.

4

Frankie's Dream

Frankie lay on top of the bed with his clothes on. He was too tired to peel down the blankets and get in, too tired even to take his magic shoes off. Still, his blood was singing. He was too excited to sleep. "Hyper" was what his mother always said on Christmas and birthdays when the kids started spinning like tops and couldn't stop, until they collapsed on the floor with a crash.

His head was swimming. The room, full of sisters snoring gently and bits of tin foil sparkling in the moonlight, was a smear of colour and shine, like a fancy bathroom he saw one time, or a marble cake, or the swirl pictures he remembered doing in kindergarten.

His mind was jammed with pictures, and it was making him feel sick, like the time they smoked comics, and the other time they took the beer from the fridge at Odie's house.

He tried with his eyes open and his eyes shut, imagining the pattern on the ceiling. "Let me sleep," he said out loud and inside his head, and soon he heard the noise of a hundred bathtubs draining at once.

He was standing on a flat rock under the waterfall. The water was cool and comfortable and his skin felt nice. Rainbows danced in the light.

He liked the sound of water rushing and slapping itself on the rocks, making a path from one side of the river to the other, from a forest full of singing birds to a field of wildflowers. There was so much colour, his eyes were singing pleasantly.

He felt his arms and legs growing, and he wasn't sure if it were his magic or if there were something special in the spray that covered him like a tent of shooting stars.

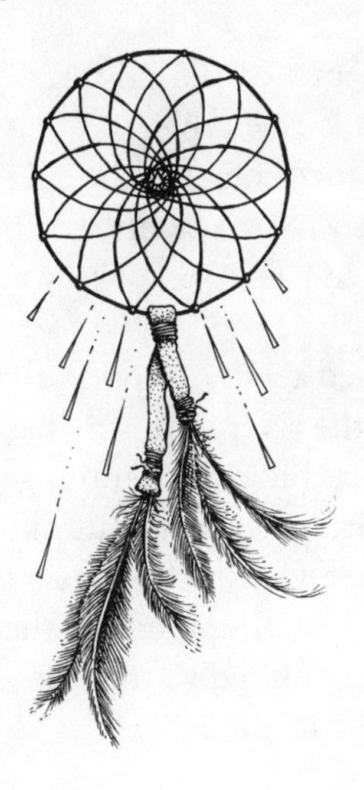

It was as if enormous hands had taken hold of him and pulled everywhere. He felt like a piece of playdough being stretched into something bigger and different. Something was helping him change from a short and chubby kid to a man with arms and legs strong enough to swim in a river with hurrying water.

There was no one else. Except for the birds and animals watching his transformation from boy to man, he was alone. No parents, no elders or uncles and aunties, no friends or brother and sisters to witness the miracle of his change. He felt strange and new, but not the littlest bit lonely. He knew he would find the others later, when this part was over.

Stepping out of his glittering shower into the sunlight, Frankie felt his toes on the edge of the rock. He pushed his hands against the sky and stretched. He was a human tent pole holding it all up. He yawned. The sun was warm on his shoulders.

He listened to the birds as they nested in trees bending into the river, and smelled air fragrant with wild grasses in bloom, humming with millions of tiny insects. Branches sang out like windchimes hitting each other gently the way his sisters, sharing the big iron bed, bumped in their sleep without waking up. It sounded to him like angels flying low and whispering in the leaves.

A cockatiel with red cheeks and yellow feathers landed on Frankie's shoulder and pushed its beak through his streaming hair. "Fly, fly," he heard it say and he moved his arms even though he did not believe it was possible and lifted off and soared, as the little bird hung on to him like a fantastic earring, only letting go when Frankie finally bent his new man's body forward, shut his arms in front of him, and cut into the water with a small neat splash.

The water moved like a subway full of fish in incredible neon jackets, creatures that slid by, ignoring him, opening and shutting their mouths, releasing bubbles that rose and burst on the turbulent surface of the stream. Frankie imitated them, and found he also had the gift of breathing underwater.

He was as sleek and graceful as a fish on a train speeding underground, and dizzy with the pleasure of it.

I can fly! I can swim! He hardly had time to think of the words as the water carried him in its liquid arms out to sea. I have seen the top of the world! He wanted to shout to his own shadow passing over smooth rocks and sand. I have seen the top and the bottom and the in-between! He was laughing underwater, the silent laugh of a happy fish.

"I am good magic," he said to himself. He didn't look where he was going, shut his eyes, breathed out and the bubbles propelled him right into the open jaws of a giant clam.

The door shut tight, before Frankie had time to think and he was shut in, in a kind of moonlit darkness, feeling the slippery walls of his iridescent room. It was as if the edges were strung with fairy lights, which he realized were pearls— enough, he guessed, for a whole string. He wanted to gather them up and, because he was naked in this dream, save them in his cheeks.

So many times he had stopped in front of the jewelry-store window to look at the pearls in their blue velvet boxes. They would be so beautiful on his mother's brown skin.

His father worked hard fishing in the summer and carving in the winter, but there was never enough money left over after buying food and making payments on the camper to buy nice things for his mother. And she used all her sweater money to buy clothes for the children.

Is it stealing, he wondered, if I am in a dream?

Maybe I am supposed to take them. He tried to take a step. The silky insides of the clam felt like the waterbed in Odie's parent's bedroom. He fell and landed in a moving softness. It was a dream in which he couldn't move.

One by one, the lights went out and Frankie felt caressed by the warmth of tiny light bulbs. His head filled with a strange heaviness, as if each pearl brought with it the burden of sleep. He closed his eyes and yawned, still waiting for the magic to finish growing inside him. He put his thumb in his mouth, the way he had when he was a baby, and fell asleep.

In the dream inside his dream, he moved on his lovely cushion through fathoms of starfish and glowing underwater plants and, as he floated, he grew even bigger, until he filled the clamshell.

Eventually, it became uncomfortable and he woke up, his arms and legs cramped and sore, his eyes filled with sand. He moved and bumped his head against the hard shell, the way a bird does. He wanted to touch it to see if there was a lump, but he couldn't move. It was such a tight fit.

Slowly the shell opened to reveal a crack of light and the sound of waves on a beach. Frankie pushed his fingers toward the light and something grabbed them and pulled.

He screamed. There was a terrible pain. The light hurt his eyes and the noise became unbearable.

"Get up, Frankie. You're late for school again." All three sisters were talking and pulling at him at once.

He stood up, wobbling on fuzzy legs and knew he smelled like the sea. His clothes were damp. They seemed to have shrunk. Circles of light plopped from his lap and rolled under the bed, into the carpet, into the greedy hands of several little girls. "Look," one cried. "It's pearls!"

5

How a Bad Morning Turns Out

For Odie it was a rotten morning. He hadn't said anything to Jen and Frankie the night before, but, when he left the house, his parents had been fighting about money. The trouble had started with the phone bill. Jen had heard about a teen line you could call. When you dialed the number, there were all kinds of kids talking at once. The only problem was that it was long distance.

Over Thanksgiving weekend, they'd had a hundred and thirty dollars worth of conversation with total strangers. When Odie's dad found out, he hit the roof. His mum said he didn't mean to be bad, and besides it was all her fault, because he was a spoiled only child. She was crying and his dad was yelling and telling her it was a miracle Odie was such a brain, when he had a mother who was so dumb she didn't even notice when she was being manipulated by a self-absorbed little brat.

When Odie was tiptoeing down the fire escape the night before, he stopped and listened at his parents' window. They were still arguing in bed. He knew he was going to get it in the morning, and he had a terrible sleep after he returned from the graveyard in the first light of morning and crawled back up the ladder to his bed.

In his dream, his mother was thirty feet tall and totally muscular. She was standing in the kitchen with her head poking through the roof and crying so hard the room filled up with water. When she picked Odie and his dad up, one in each hand, so they wouldn't drown, she squeezed so hard on their ribs they could feel their bones cracking.

Neither of them protested, because you can't do that in a dream. The words won't come. Besides, they were out of breath from being squished in her mighty hands. When the phone and the doorbell both rang at once, she just stood there holding them. The ringing went on and on in their spinning heads.

When the alarm went off and his face was attacked by dogbreath at seven a.m., his mother and father were still snoring in their beds. He got up as quietly as he could, put the dog out to pee and made his own breakfast and lunch.

Then, absent-mindedly pouring milk on his cereal so the bowl overflowed, he remembered he had left the bath water running. It took every towel in the linen closet to soak up the mess on the bathroom floor and, by the time he got back to his breakfast, it was so soggy he fed it to his dog, who wasn't fussy about what he ate.

It was a cold day. He stuck his nose outside, then went back in the house and put on the military greatcoat he bought at the army surplus store with the birthday money his grandpa sent from Vancouver in a card that said, like always, "Sorry I forgot your birthday."

Odie bought a super coat with two rows of shiny brass buttons. It came right down to his ankles. He was really lucky to get it. Most of the army surplus came in way bigger sizes, but this time it was almost perfect. His mum liked it, because it was warm, and Grandpa sent an answer to his thank-you letter that was full of stories about the war in the old days before Odie was even a tadpole swimming around inside Wonder Woman.

He never thought the other kids wouldn't think it was cool. Lots of them wore cami-pants and other stuff they bought second hand or found in trunks in their attics. When he reached the playground that morning, Joey Small, the biggest bully in Grade seven, called him a Russian spy and spat on him.

Odie's arms were full of books and the bag full of Oreos he packed for his lunch and he was wearing new glasses he didn't dare break, so, instead of getting in a fight with Joey, who was bigger anyway, he called him a name.

Odie's tongue was his strongest muscle, and he was famous for the quality of his insults. Sometimes kids gave him candy or baseball cards just for telling somebody off for them. He was their mouthpiece. Words came easily to him because his grandfather was a lawyer.

Unfortunately, he was careless that morning of little sleep and he forgot to look around first. Mr. Smith heard every word from his window, which he kept open in every kind of weather just for the purpose of spying, and he ran to the office to report to Mr. Willis, the principal, who put Odie's name in the Black Book and wanted to see him right away. "I hope you catch it in your zipper!" Odie yelled to Joey over his shoulder as he felt himself being yarded by his collar up the front stairs and down the hall to the office.

He didn't care. His life was a train wreck anyway.

For sure his mother was going to get even with him after school. Bodybuilders hate to cry and he would be the one to pay for her humiliation. There would be liver and lumpy mashed potatoes for dinner and he would have to scoop the dog's love offerings off the lawn, or worse.

It wasn't so bad in the office with Mr. Willis. Everyone knew he was a wimp who didn't have the guts to punish kids or get rid of teachers like Mr. Smith, no matter how horrible they were. He sat at his messy desk patting Pusscat, the school ratmuncher, a "boy" who had seven kittens last spring. Mr. Willis told Odie he should watch his language. He didn't like swearing on the school grounds and he wasn't going to allow it.

By the time Odie had hung up his coat and put away his lunch, he had blamed all his troubles on Jen. The long distance phone calls, which had been the beginning of his very bad day, were her dumb idea and she probably slept like a baby when she got home from the graveyard.

"What's wrong with you, Odie? You look like a bear that ate mouse poison." Jen was blooming. She held up her hands.

Her warts were gone. As he suspected, she had an okay sleep after she crawled back in her window and her mother, who woke up in an unusually good mood because she won at Bingo the night before, had made her waffles with frozen strawberries and whipped cream for breakfast.

"Don't want to talk." He sulked past her and sat down at his place, only somebody had moved his chair and he landed on the floor.

Odie's tailbone hurt like crazy. It felt like some Nazi Stormtrooper backed the bottom of his spine into an electric fence. He tried not to cry, but his glasses sort of fogged up.

Frankie, who was carefully unwrapping his last toffee, gave him a sympathetic look, which meant to say he'd give him another if he had it.

"Good morning, class." Mr. Smith was feeling great after taking Odie to the office. He slammed the window shut, his spying finished. No point wasting fresh air on degenerate kids. "Instead of gym this morning, we're going to do spelling."

Odie groaned. He was dyslexic and couldn't spell at all except the way the words sounded to him. Because he was super smart in every other way, Mr. Smith wouldn't believe there was anything wrong with him. He told the school psychologist Odie was a manipulative little monster who spelled words wrong on purpose, just to confuse teachers.

It wasn't true. Odie would have given anything to be able to remember the way the letters were supposed to go.

"Get to the board, Ormonde," the cruel pedagogue hissed, pointing his finger at the tip of Odie's nose.

His heart sank. He'd never get it right. Even the kids who liked him would laugh. They couldn't help it.

He picked up the chalk with wooden fingers.

"Spell Onomatopoeia." There was a cruel smile teasing the corners of his mouth. "Hurry up."

Jen was mouthing the letters from her desk, but Odie didn't look at her. His mind was a muddle. In a panic, he wrote whatever came into his head. O-N-A-M-A-T-A-P-E-A.

Nobody laughed this time. Nobody was sure how to spell it. No one except Jen.

"Wrong!" Mr. Smith shouted joyfully and reached for his ruler. "Put out your hands!"

Odie put them out automatically, even though he knew a teacher was supposed to phone your parents before giving corporal punishment. His mother probably would have said yes anyway, once she had seen the mess he made in the bathroom that morning and considering the trouble he was already in, despite the fact she hated Mr. Smith too and tried to start a petition to get him fired.

Odie looked at Frankie and pleaded with his eyes. Maybe he could do something now. The warts vanished, didn't they?

Everyone in the class squirmed with remembered pain. For a little bald jerk, Mr. Smith was very strong, especially if you were the first. When lots of kids were in trouble, they all tried to be last in line so he was tired out before he got to them.

Frankie wasn't looking. He had his left index finger on the middle of his forehead, where his third eye was supposed to be, and he was concentrating.

Odie pulled back his hands, took off his glasses and rubbed his eyes. He wanted to see perfectly. Jen's mouth was opened so wide a hummingbird could have flown in and taken her tonsils.

The whole class was looking at Frankie, who was changing colours and making weird choking noises, his finger still pressed on the magic spot.

Mr. Smith was angry now. No one was paying attention to him. He smacked his ruler down on the front desk and it broke in half. Nobody noticed or jumped like they usually did. He had broken seven rulers already this term. All eyes were on Frankie, who was having a fit.

Mr. Smith stumbled to Frankie's desk. He was losing control. Frankie's noises got louder and he was surrounded by the kind of light you see coming off neon at night. Mr. Smith was a rainbow of rage. He was just reaching for the spot between Frankie's neck and shoulderblade that completely paralyzed him with pain without leaving a mark, when he started to vanish.

He was becoming something else, goo that dripped on the floor and disappeared. His bald head, beaky nose and terrible breath all melted away with the chalk-covered blue suit.

"Oh, look!" Jen was on top of her desk, pointing. Frankie had done it. "Frankie's vanished him!"

While all the cheering and laughing was going on, Odie had a weird feeling in his stomach and it had nothing to do with missing breakfast. How could such a bad day turn out so well? He couldn't believe his luck.

6

In Which the Kids Have a New Problem

No sooner had Frankie whispered magic words into the palm of his hand than an amazingly beautiful parrot rose out of the vanishing muck that used to be Mr. Smith, and shook its wings. It also was wearing a blue suit and yellow tie. That is, its feathers were mostly blue, except for a bit of yellow under the throat.

The bird rose with a shriek, circled the room four times, nearly touching the fluorescent lights in the ceiling, then landed on Jen's shoulder and pecked at the tiny gold earring her father had sent for her last birthday.

The class was in pandemonium. This didn't seem to ruffle the bird, who was quite content on his cosy perch. It did bother Odie. Everyone was talking at once. Some people were leaping out of their desks, knocking over their chairs in the excitement. He stood up on a desk and held out his arms. "Shut-up, everybody. Please be quiet."

It seemed to take the longest time to cut through the din, but Odie persisted. Reluctantly, the kids abandoned their noise and turned their attention to him.

"They're going to hear us down at the office, and then they'll come. We'll be in the most terrible trouble. We made Mr. Smith disappear," he said, as if everyone didn't know it.

"Not WE," said Melanie Barker, the class goodie-two-shoes, former favourite of Mr. Smith. "Frankie did it. I saw him and I heard him and I'm going to tell." She rose like a ship under full sail, her lace crinolines swishing and hitting the desks, sending homework papers flying, and made for the door, but not as fast as Jenny, who tackled her just as her hand was reaching for the knob.

With Jen and the bird on top of her, Melanie

couldn't move. A cheer went up as Jen kept her pinned and Odie struggled to keep control of the crowd. Nobody liked Melanie. She was mean and hurt people's feelings and she always had to be the best at everything. If somebody beat her on a test or ran faster in a race, she had a snit and sulked for days.

Some kids sucked up to her around the end of the month when she got parcels full of toffee from her grandparents in England, but not Jen and Frankie and Odie. They'd rather starve.

"Stop the racket," Odie begged. "We could all go to jail."

"But Melanie said . . ." Lisa Wood insisted.

"Melanie, Schmelanie. Don't you understand? We all wished it. Even her. If we didn't wish it, Frankie wouldn't have had the power to do it."

"Is Frankie a wizard?" Jim Crosby wanted to know. He was reading a library book about Merlin, the magician. It was the story of King Arthur and the Knights of the Round Table. His head was busy as a beehive when the clover blooms. If Frankie had magic powers, just think what they could become, the whole class, all Sirs and Lords and Ladies helping people in distress and getting medals and being interviewed on the six o'clock news.

"Frankie has special powers he got from his late uncle. It has to do with being an Indian. He's sort of a medicine man."

"Well then, make him bring Mr. Smith back." Melanie was wriggling under Jen's powerful grip. "I don't want to get in trouble."

"Be quiet, Melanie. You're just a big bag of air." Odie didn't want her to mix things up. The class had to stick together. "Listen, we haven't hurt Mr. Smith. We've just put him on ice until the end of the year." Odie crossed all his fingers and toes. Oboy, did he ever hope that was the truth. If anything really terrible happened to their teacher, they were in for it.

"Buck up, boys." A rasping voice cut through Odie's speech, and everyone realized the parrot, now off Jenny's shoulder and perched on Mr. Smith's desk, could speak.

"He'll tell on us," somebody said what they were all thinking, even the ones with delayed thoughts. It was obvious. The parrot still had Mr. Smith's brain and his powers of speech. He could be as much trouble to them now as ever.

"No, he won't," Odie replied quickly, although he had a hard time thinking of a reason why that couldn't happen. "Besides, no one would take him seriously. Who'd believe it?"

Everybody fell silent.

"What do we call him?"

Frankie stood up and spoke for the first time since the magic incantation. He glowed like a god. There was light all around his body. Jen thought of the plastic goose in her room with a 25 watt tummy that made her feel safe at night. Frankie had the same effect on her.

"Call him 'Mr. Smith'. Except around grown-ups. If you name him in front of them, he might become real again and whup the living daylights out of us." He looked around the room. "All of us. And as for you Melanie and anyone else with the stupid idea of becoming a tattle-tale, you will become something else if you even open your ugly mouths to tell. I will see to it." Frankie sat down with the puffy sound of a balloon emptying. He had never made such a big important speech before in his life.

"Frankie is right," Odie said. "We have to stick together or we'll all be up the creek. If we keep quiet, nobody gets hurt." He made a menacing face at Melanie, who was quite capable of letting down the group to get herself out of the mud.

"What are we going to tell them, Odie?" Jen asked.

"We'll tell them practically nothing. That way our stories will be the same. Mr. Smith left the room, that's all. Maybe he had to pee or sneak a cigarette. And he never came back." Odie made a pretend sad face and everybody laughed.

"Bad boy," the bird said. He looked like he wanted to add more, but he kept on repeating, "Bad boy. Bad boy."

"What about the parrot?" Sherry, the class historian, wanted to know. "How do we explain him? He didn't just appear out of thin air."

"We'll say he flew in the window." Odie was inspired. "We'll advertise in Lost and Found, but since he doesn't belong to anybody, no one will turn up to claim him. I think we should keep him here until we're ready to change him back."

"When will that be?" Jen was worrying about Mr. Smith's daughter again. Even if he was as mean a father as he was a teacher, a mean father was better than no father at all. That meant nobody's feet to stand on and dance when you played records, nobody to make french toast on Saturday morning, or say I love you that special way when they tucked you in at night, nobody to push your hair back from your forehead when you were throwing up after you pigged out at a birthday party.

"That will be someday," said Odie mysteriously. How did he know how it was going to turn out? How could he read Jen's thoughts and make her feel better? He wasn't Frankie Zapper. Odie was just a plain ordinary person with a very high I.Q.

7

Odie Reveals a Terrible Threat

"My parents are so boring," Odie whispered into his Garfield phone. "They're always reading books about meaningful relationships and raising an only child so he isn't a moron and junk like that. Do you want to hear the new scam?"

"Nope." Frankie didn't want to think about

anything unpleasant. His stomach was full of boiled potatoes and salmon and he felt like burping.

"What was that?" Odie asked.

"I burped."

"Get serious, Frankie. I've got big trouble."

"Whenever you've got trouble, I have to put my neck in a sling. I wish you'd just scribble all your problems on a scrap of paper and then burn it without showing it to anybody, me especially."

"Listen. They want to send me to boarding school, so I can learn to live with other kids."

Oh ginger peachy. Odie got him into this big mess and now he was going to fly off on a magic carpet to some snobby place where rich kids learned to eat with a knife and fork.

"That's great. You really made my day." Frankie squelched another eruption from his stomach.

"I don't like it any more than you do," Odie said. "I'd have to leave you guys and my experiments, and the school would probably force me to play some dumb game where the other team gets points for breaking your bones and your glasses." Odie was forgetting to whisper. "It would be just my luck to share a room with some person who snored."

"Yah." Frankie was feeling kind of sadistic. "I hear everybody snores at boarding school and you never get any sleep. After a while it drives you crazy. Also, they make you run in the rain and if you do anything wrong they beat your butt with a paddle. And," he added, "the food is terrible. They give you nothing but porridge. Everybody gets real fat and covered with zits."

Odie groaned. Nobody had ever spanked him before or made him eat porridge. Frankie knew all about residential schools because his mum had to go to one when she was a girl. She got strapped if she spoke her own language and she only got to go back to see her parents on the reserve during summer holidays. "I'm not going," he said. "I refuse."

"Right, Odie. G'bye." Frankie hung up quickly, before Odie had anything more to say. He needed to think. It was all happening so fast.

They'd had an awful day at school. When Mr. Smith didn't show up in the staff room at lunch time, Mr. Willis came down to their classroom to check. Frankie was sure the end of the world was coming. When they were asked what had happened to their teacher, Mr. Smith squawked and flapped his wings, which made Mr. Willis totally spaz out.

"Who brought that damned bird to school?" Odie, hearing the swear word, caught Mr. Willis' eye and smirked and Mr. Willis turned an even deeper shade of purple. "Well?" he raged.

Melanie stood up, straightened the lace collar on her blouse and Frankie's heart did a swan dive in an empty swimmimg pool. "The bird flew in the window, Mr. Willis, and we decided to look after it until somebody claimed it. We thought there might be a reward and we could put it in the school orphan fund."

What a liar! Mr. Willis was proud of the money they earned in car washes and spellathons to send to their foster child in Colombia. He said his school was the best because his kids were willing to work to help others with less than they had.

Melanie was brilliant, a real honest to goodness sociopath, with no conscience whatsoever. Her only thought was saving her own skin. They had to hand it to her. She was quite an actress and she really knew how to suck.

"Well, Melanie," Mr. Willis calmed down considerably. "That's a very good idea. I'm going to put you in charge of the class until Mr. Smith comes back from wherever it was he went. Where did you say he went?" Nobody said. They just hoped Mr. Willis forgot they hadn't told him. It was pretty clear to them he was flying with only one wing.

Melanie had her way and the rest of the day was pretty intolerable. Her bossy voice gave Frankie a headache and he needed to get to his room to count some zaps and go on a nice relaxing trip.

As he rode home on his rusty three-speed bike, listening to the horrible noise of his pedal hitting his chain guard, bent in a recent collision with a large and vicious dog that seemed to have it in for paper boys and Indian kids because he never chased anybody else's bicycle, he had an intuition his mother was making cookies.

He closed his eyes and smelled chocolate chips melting in her fragrant oven.

A car honked. Frankie had ridden through a stop sign almost into the path of a Coca Cola delivery truck. There was a terrible sound of burning rubber and a thousand bottles clinking together. He got off his bike and said sorry to the driver who told him to watch out. He could lose his job for squish-

ing a kid, even if it wasn't his fault. He had seven of his own and he didn't want to be responsible for killing any.

What a day. Melanie was the Queen Bag, he almost got hit by a truck and he just knew there was more to come, even if his head was full of the smell of warm cookies.

After they finished talking, he hung up the phone and tried to forget Odie's terrible news. It was up to Odie to convince his parents they were entertaining a catastrophe. Frankie had enough to worry about without facing the prospect of being deserted under fire. If Odie went to that snob school, Frankie might as well be buried alive beside his uncle Joe. A guy needed a buddy, or life wasn't worth living.

He shuffled into the kitchen, grabbed a handful of cookies, went to his room and lay down on his bed. His dad was out stacking firewood at the bighouse and his sisters were sitting around the kitchen stove with his mother carding wool. Frankie's zaps glowed in the light from the moon and the crack under the door. He emptied his head and started to count.

He found a circle of thirteen zaps and concentrated on the centre. It became an unblinking eye and he fell into the pupil through a long black tunnel with smooth sides. The falling was warm and pleasant, not too fast. It became morning, that time just before the sun slips into the sky when it is hard to tell where the light begins and darkness ends.

From the edges of his dream came a great blue cloud. It was birds, thousands of them, shrieking. As they came closer and he could tell one from the other, he could see they were identical blue parrots with yellow throats.

As the birds moved toward him, they split down the middle and formed a circle, not a one-dimensional circle, but a formation like a sphere.

As Frankie turned in his weightlessness, he realized he was the centre of a living ball. He was a bird without wings inside a beautiful cage. As he rolled closer to the sun, the squawking gave way to a louder silence and the colours became almost unbearably beautiful, like stained glass on a very bright day.

Frankie, almost blinded by the intense light, watched the parrot faces become human, Mr. Smith reflected in ten thousand mirrors. "Watch out," sang the mouths in unison.

"I'm sorry. I'm sorry," Frankie cried out, as the heavenly light faded, and the birds became birds again as he fell into a fitful sleep.

Jen stood in the doorway looking at her friend, who lay on his bed muttering, his mouth smeared with chocolate and little dark crumbs.

It was only seven o'clock at night. "He's asleep," she said, unnecessarily, to herself, because

Frankie wasn't listening and his mother and sisters were chatting and laughing noisily in the kitchen.

They offered her tea when she pulled up a chair and sat beside them, warming her hands beside the wood stove. Frankie's mum put in lots of cream and sugar, without even asking how she liked it. She just knew. Her own mum drank her tea raw which Jen figured might be the reason for her crabbiness. Her stomach was probably full of bitter stuff that hurt the same as when you got your period, which Jen knew about because she had just recently grown up.

"Anything happen at school today?" Mrs. Zapper asked. "My son sure was in a bad mood when he came home."

"Not really," Jen answered, reaching for a cookie.

8

Life With a Substitute Teacher

The new substitute was an android from the planet Nerd. She wore an ugly black hairpiece that didn't match her real colour and slipped all over the place in spite of about three dozen bobby pins that popped off into space whenever she jiggled her brain, shoes that had walked out of a swamp, and a dress that was knit by a monkey with a nervous disorder.

She knew she was sub number seven, and had been acting like a hired assassin for the four-and-one-half days she'd lasted, so far. It was Friday, and she hadn't smiled once during a week of screaming and detentions and double grammar periods.

She was bad, but her nasty demeanour was an inspiration to the class. Never before, even with Mr. Smith, had they been so united in their determination to sabotage a teacher. They would find a way to get rid of her, short of turning her into a feathered friend for Mr. Smith. Frankie refused to do any more transformations, and who could blame him? Nobody really wanted to attract suspicion, and a second disappearance was sure to start some kind of terrible inquisition that would result in a lot of twelve year olds being made into chopped liver or wieners for the Sunday School picnic.

So far, the grown-ups seemed to think Mr. Smith was just a weirdo who had taken off on some unplanned holiday, and not the helpless victim of kidpower gone berserk. Frankie was right. They shouldn't press their luck. Any more disappearances would be sure to attract unwanted attention.

Ms. Take was the sub's name, and everyone agreed her blood had been drained and replaced with lemon juice. They were working up some really bad karma for Ms. Take who, as yet, hadn't reacted to tacks on her chair or cartoons on the blackboard. She just kept on with her ruthless, boring teaching, while the boys and girls schemed and smirked and encouraged Mr. Smith, who was jealous of every substitute, to torture her.

After lunch on Friday, Ms. Take noticed a half-eaten Granny Smith apple sitting on the corner of Jen's desk. Before Jen could say a word, Ms. Take screamed something about children starving in the third world and spoiled brats in North America only eating half an apple before they threw it out. Jen was trying to protest, but Ms. Take had already grabbed the piece of fruit and gobbled it, core and all, little bits of bubbly saliva dripping from the corners of her scarlet-painted mouth. "Ms. Take, Ms. Take," Jen finally got it out. "Mr. Sm . . . , I mean the parrot pooped on the apple. That's why I didn't eat it."

Ms. Take, realizing what she had done, instantly turned a revolting shade of blue, the class went totally berserk and Mr. Smith, enjoying the ensuing riot, flew to the poisoned substitute and sat on her shoulder.

"Get off," she hissed. He was pecking at a hideous earring that looked like a giant fish hook and was probably an exquisite instrument of torture, her last resort when every other classroom punishment failed. She was spitting bits of half-chewed apple on the floor and slapping at his feathers.

Mr. Smith, not taking too well to corporal punishment, which he had never thought twice about handing out in his previous incarnation, bit her neck hard, and flew off, whistling, to the top of the bookshelf.

Ms. Take completely lost her cool and chased after him. She tried to climb the bookshelf, and her stockings, responding to the unbearable strain of her excessive weight, popped a leak and let out little ribbons of runaway fat.

"Her stockings ran!" Jen shouted, as if everybody hadn't noticed already. Ms. Take made a deep horrible sound like a bear that had been shot and wounded and, holding onto the shelf with one hand, hurled a book at Mr. Smith, who simply flew back to his desk and waited there with a contented smile on his beak.

Ms. Take puffed back to the front of the classroom. She stood in her torn stockings and unruly wig, which was threatening to cover her left eye entirely, and tried to catch her breath. Everyone stopped laughing and talking and waited for her to speak.

"Either it leaves, or I do." She waited through two minutes of nervous silence, while everyone tried not to laugh, then walked out of the room two hours early, slamming the door so hard behind her the chalk jumped on the blackboard shelf.

Victory! The class held a vote and Odie counted hands. Democracy, at last. They decided to do art, and it was unanimous. All of them wanted to draw Mr. Smith, who was becoming quite popular in his present form.

9

Mr. Smith Disappears and Pusscat is a Suspect

SuperJen, her red hair flying, came down the school steps in one jump, ran three giant steps and just about knocked Frankie and Odie, who were taking baby steps across the schoolyard, seeing who could be last to class, right off their runners.

"He's gone!" she grabbed Frankie by the tops of his arms and nearly shook his face off. "He's gone!"

Odie felt the blood crawl out of his head and thump in his heart. He knew what was coming, but he didn't want to believe it. "Who's gone?" he asked.

"Mr. Smith. He isn't in the room. And Pusscat is there. Somebody let him, uh her, in."

"Mr. Smith wouldn't let Pusscat eat him, Jen. He'd fly to the roof and he'd bite and scream. Pusscat's a wimp. She doesn't have the guts to fight Mr. Smith."

"Oh yeah? You come and see."

Their stomachs churning like cement mixers

full of rotten regurgitated breakfast, Frankie and Odie followed Jen up the stairs and down the hall to 6A. There was no sign of Ms. Take, who was at an early appointment to have her moustache removed, or so they figured when she turned up later with a red mark where there used to be bristles.

A sad tangle of kids moped around Mr. Smith's desk. In the centre was Pusscat wearing a blue feather in her whiskers, and a very contented smile. Nobody was patting her. She/he stood up, stretched and gave her/himself a congratulatory lick.

"Murderer!" Melanie shrieked and the cat jumped off the desk and found a warm spot near the radiator. “Mr. Smith is dead. This stupid cat did it and it’s all your fault.” She pointed at Frankie and he noticed her tear-filled eyes looked like wobbly mud. Melanie was a pig. As if he didn’t feel bad enough already.

“Now what are we gonna do?” Jen thumped into her seat and put her hands under her chin, her only thinking position.

“Maybe he’ll come back as something else,” Frankie suggested. “Maybe his soul’s gone into Pusscat.”

Hearing her name mentioned, Pusscat perked up his/her ears. A purr escaped from her lipstick grey mouth. She was the centre of attention.

“Okay,” Odie said. “Let’s think. It’s possible Puss ate Mr. Smith, but not likely. Mr. Smith would be very hard for a cat to catch.”

“I bet he’d taste terrible, too,” Frankie added.

“Second, Ms. Take might have come back and taken him somewhere. Maybe to a pet store or one of her friends.”

“He’d never let her take him alive,” Stew Cropper observed.

“Maybe. Maybe not,” Odie answered. “She could have got him when he was sleeping or given him some drug.” He was thinking of hankies soaked in chloroform like he’d seen in the movies when people got kidnapped and taken away in the trunks of cars or two-seater airplanes so they could be interrogated deep in the jungle, or in criminal offices in sewers under the city.

"Another possibility is Frankie's suggestion that Mr. Smith has simply changed again. He might have been uncomfortable with his blue suit. We should check around the room and look for anything suspicious."

Thirty vitamin-charged adolescents sprang to action. They had to find him. The room was being torn apart.

When Ms. Take arrived a few minutes later, wearing a different wig and the same ugly dress, the class was busy at their work, counting goldfish and cleaning the hamster cage, looking for signs of an unusual new baby, possibly blue, anything bald or smelling faintly of onion and cigarettes.

"I'm glad that bird's gone," she muttered and almost smiled as Pusscat sauntered out the door and headed for the lunch room, drawn by the lovely smell of peanut butter and banana sandwiches left in the garbage cans—a nice dessert, the kids thought, after raw parrot.

"Take your seats, please."

Worry and concern was making the room stuffy, but the kids knew the only one allowed to open the window was Mr. Smith himself, and then only before and after school and during lunch and recess when he wanted to spy on the kids and hear what they had to say about him and other things that would get them into trouble, the worst kind of trouble being the dreaded Black Book that sat in a locked drawer in Mr. Willis' desk.

That book could ruin their lives, Mr. Smith assured the kids. When they grew up, they would still be haunted by childhood crimes. Black marks in the Black Book could keep them out of university or stop them from getting jobs or getting married. What woman would marry a man who was in the Black Book for chasing a little girl with a snake in Grade five? What firm would hire a boy who drove a foul ball right through the kindergarten window? The answer was: none. They were paralysed with fear of the Black Book.

Odie couldn't breathe. He was going to flaunt the rules. He got out of his desk without permission and went to the curtains that separated the class from the outside world. He parted them, and his mouth fell open. A window was already open. So that was it. Mr. Smith had gone to see the world.

10

The Search

"Oh Odie, I'm scared. I'll bet he's frozen to death." Jen blew on her fingers and shivered. It had never snowed in October before, not for as long as she could remember. They were walking home from school, listening to cars slipping out of control on the slick streets. Nobody was ready for this unseasonably cold weather.

Odie didn't know much about God. His parents didn't believe in that stuff. Sometimes he wondered, though, about things like miracles and stuff like airplanes falling out of the sky for no reason. How did people like Frankie get special gifts if there wasn't somebody handing them out?

So much thinking made Odie's head ache. It was like wondering where the universe began and ended and what would happen if a star landed in your garden or put itself out in your swimming pool, if you happened to have one. Odie had only had the plastic kind when he was little. His mother was always telling him not to pee in it, but, of course, he did because it was warm and cosy and he forgot.

It was not warm and cosy today. Jen and Odie were only wearing their jean jackets because the morning had looked bright and sunny before storm clouds rolled in. They wondered if Mr. Smith was shivering, too, in his tropical clothes, minus the feathers Pusscat picked up in their classroom rampage. Usually the kids loved snow. It gave them a chance to gang up on the bullies and wash their faces. Best of all was when school got cancelled, because the teachers were too lame to clear their driveways and drive to school.

"Do you think he opened the window himself?" Jen asked. "Maybe he remembered how to do it. When Pusscat bugged him and bugged him, maybe he just decided to open the window and leave?"

"If he was that smart, Jen, then he would know

enough to find a warm dry spot to hide out in."

"Maybe he went to Hawaii or South America." They were studying the Amazon in Socials. Jen was doing a report on the jungle, which was being destroyed by greedy businessmen. "Oh no!" she remembered. "He can't go there." Tears appeared on her cheeks and Odie thought he could see them freezing.

"Don't forget, Jen, Mr. Smith isn't an ordinary parrot. He was made by magic and he has all kinds of special powers."

"Like what?" Jen asked, morosely.

"Like human stuff. He can go to a restaurant, or drive a car."

"Who ever heard of a bird driving a car?" Jen kicked what looked like snow and turned out to be a rock covered by snow. "Ouch!"

"He opened a window, didn't he?"

"Odie, we think he opened the window. Maybe he opened the window. Just because you say something might have happened doesn't make it true."

He had to agree. Jennifer was getting logical in her old age. Maybe she was going to turn into a sensible person after all, someone he could trust as much as Frankie, who was reasonable about everything and knew when to keep his lips zipped together.

The class had drawn a map and divided the

little town into areas for searching. They drew partners and Jen and Odie got each other. The idea was that one could look left, while the other looked right and up and down, and so forth and so on. They were determined to cover every square inch of the snow- covered landscape.

"Mr. Smith?" Jen stood under a tree beside the sidewalk and called. "Are you up there? 'Cause if you are, it isn't fair. You're making us all upset and I'm missing my karate lesson, and I'm cold." She stamped her feet. "Come down now!"

"Jen!" She was embarrassing him. Odie wanted to make himself invisible when a teenager he knew walked by and made a sign to his girlfriend that the girl standing on the pavement talking to a tree had probably fallen out of one herself, and cracked her head.

"Mr. Smith isn't up there."

"How do you know?"

"Because the tree is bare and I can't see him in the branches. Mr. Smith doesn't have camouflage. Why would he sit in this stupid tree anyway? It's practically in the middle of the traffic. All he could do up there is count cars and smell exhaust. He isn't that dumb."

"How do you know? You think you're so smart, Odie. You think you know everything. I'm tired of being bossed around." Jen was getting mad. Her foot came out before she had time to think about it. She curled her shoe around his calf and tripped him, and they both went crashing in the snow. Neither of them had mitts or hats, and their fingers and ears were cold.

"I hate you. I hate you." Jen was really crying now. She was making awful moo sounds. Her face, pushed into his, because she landed on top, was plum coloured and her nose was dribbling. Odie thought she looked like a grape that had sprung a leak.

"You knocked my glasses off, Jen," he said. "And they're very expensive. You'd have to babysit Marge Burple's kids for fifty-seven hours to pay for some new ones."

Odie knew Jen hated looking after the Burple kids. They were awful, the house was a pigpen and the fridge a wasteland, never even a crumb of anything worthwhile to eat. Everytime she sat there for more than a couple of hours she got hungry and ordered a pizza, which took all her babysitting money, and her allowance besides.

Worse, Marge always had a large bill she couldn't break, a twenty or a fifty, sometimes even a hundred. You always had to wait forever to get paid, and there were no tips for scraping the mould off last week's dishes. Odie told her not to bother with the housework, but she couldn't stand it. Her own house was as neat as a pin. How could kids go to sleep in dirty clothes and eat off slime-covered dishes? It was gross.

Odie said it wouldn't kill them, and besides he had read that people got certain diseases because they weren't used to germs.

Jen got off. She helped Odie up and found his glasses in the snow.

"I'm sorry, Odie."

"It's O.K. We're both kind of upset."

"You know," Jen said, holding his hand, and he thought how much better hers felt without warts. Her skin was smooth and soft and her fingers curled around his, and they warmed each other up. That was one part of his body that wasn't going to freeze and fall off. "I'm afraid Melanie will tell sooner or later."

"Who'd believe her?" Odie asked.

"Yeah, maybe. Sometimes I don't believe it myself."

"You didn't think your warts would go away either."

"In the end, I did, because I wished it so hard."

"Well, I think if we wish Mr. Smith back, it will happen."

"Oh, I do too." She looked down her red drippy nose at Odie with the sincerest look of a mongrel dog begging for meat at the back door of a butcher shop. "I guess. I mean, I do and I don't. If he doesn't come back, we have to feel guilty and worry about what might happen when he does or when somebody tells. If he does, then we'll get punished right away and have a very bad year at school, but at least we wouldn't be wondering all the time."

"I don't mind wondering," Odie replied, remembering his earlier thoughts about God and the weather and the beginning and the end of things. "I think it's kind of interesting.

"If you could have a wish right now, apart from Mr. Smith, what would it be?"

"French fries," Jen said without thinking, and they both laughed. Odie just happened to have two dollars in his pocket. He had won a bet with his dad, who didn't believe he would be able to keep all his mother's voracious houseplants alive while she was at a muscle-builder's convention at Harrison Hot Springs for a whole week.

They both had double gravy plus ketchup, which Odie spilled on his best shirt, his own creation, a T-shirt with a pink and green polka dot tie painted on the front. It was his idea of dressing up.

11

The Little Sister Who Died Gets in Trouble Again

Frankie and The Little Sister Who Died crawled way out on a moss-covered cedar tree that hung over the boiling river.

"Are you scared, Angel?" Angel was the name they gave her before she died twice of pneumonia and came back both times with the help of the shaman and some honky medicine.

"Course not," she said. "I'm scared of nothing." Frankie chose her to come, because she was the quietest of the sisters and the most fearless since she'd already looked God in the face and laughed.

Angel was willing to go anywhere and do anything, and she hardly ever told.

Frankie had the bad luck to draw Melanie as his partner for the search. The good news was, she got sick. He thought he could hear her throwing up in the background when he called her house to say they had to look for Mr. Smith along the river.

"She can't come," her mother told him and hung up without saying goodbye. Frankie was hoping Melanie would miss the toilet and make a disgusting mess on her mother's fancy carpet, the one no one was allowed to walk on without taking their shoes off first. The very thought made him laugh out loud and he shook the branch.

"Cut it out, Frankie." Angel was younger and small for her age, but she didn't let him get away with anything.

Frankie paid no attention. He was still thinking about Melanie. No wonder she was so snotty, with a mother who gave out toothbrushes on Halloween and never let her get dirty or wear long pants, not even in cold weather.

"How come you never wear dresses?" he asked his sister, who ignored him as he had ignored her. Her thoughts were travelling downstream with a branch she had thrown in.

They were riding the tree like horses, astride,

their feet inches above the raging water. It had rained for two full days after the snowstorm, washing all the snow away and filling the river right up to the top of the bank.

Frankie closed his eyes. The water sounded like every machine at the laundromat going at once. He loved it.

No one could get a hook or spear in that water. The river was completely opaque, full of mud washed from the shore. The fish were safe inside the storming current, moving upriver to their final destination. Soon they would make their little holes in the gravel, perform their mating dance, lay their eggs and die in peace.

All afternoon, they had been looking for Mr. Smith. Frankie was so grateful he had Angel with him because she knew how to look for things and not scare them away. There were all kinds of birds in the grove of alder and cedar that grew along the sides of the river. They saw ducks, seagulls and cormorants, even a heron and a Stellar's jay, but no parrot.

"I think he's gone to a human place," Frankie told Angel. "He's used to being in town." He remembered what a klutz Mr. Smith had been on class outings. Their teacher knew nothing about the outdoors and even wore his blue suit on a school hike up Mount Somenos. If the bird was directed by his spirit, then it was more likely he'd gone to a movie or a drive-in restaurant to pick up scraps and keep himself warm.

"Maybe he's dead," Angel reflected, not without some pleasure, because her class was next in line for the most unpopular teacher in the school. "Maybe somebody killed him with a can of Raid, or he got eaten alive by a lawn mover."

"Nobody cuts their grass in October, Angel, not even honkies." She laughed and the tree shook again.

"Careful," Frankie warned and she stopped.

"What was it like when you died?" His voice was small and serious.

"What?" She turned around and he could see she had slipped a jawbreaker into her mouth. Her teeth were black.

"Can I have one?"

"All gone," she said. It was the truth. She had just found the half-sucked lint-covered candy in her pocket when she put her hands in to warm them up.

"I said," he reminded her, "what was it like when you were dead?" He wondered if her trips to heaven and back were anything like his travels, if there was sound and colour and what kind of feelings she had.

"It was fun," Angel answered in a voice as soft as a dog's nose pushing into his hand, so he could hardly hear. "At first it was very hot and I couldn't breathe. Then it got nice. I felt like I was being picked up by a giant and carried up in the sky. It was bright and sunny and I heard lovely music like singing in the bighouse only quieter. I didn't want it to ever end."

Frankie remembered how it was for the family. His mother cried all day and all night and his father chopped wood. The aunties came to sit with his mum. They sat around the kitchen stove and made enough water to drown a whale.

They gave Angel Indian medicine and honky medicine at the same time, hoping something would work. Her mother didn't want her to go to the hospital, but in the end she had to give in, because Angel was turning blue.

All the kids lined up on the porch to say goodbye when they took her out on the stretcher. She looked so little and still, Frankie remembered he felt sick to his stomach.

It happened the same way both times.

When she got better, they had parties and ate all the food the aunties had brought for her funeral.

In the hospital, Angel got popsicles and jell-o and ice cream. The nurses told her she had been given the right name because she knew how to fly to heaven and back.

"I see him," she said suddenly, standing up on the branch. She pointed. "Over there!"

Frankie turned to look. He saw something like the colours of Mr. Smith, but he wasn't sure. The woods were dense.

"I heard him laugh," said The Little Sister Who Died and took a step toward her brother, who was closest to the shore.

The wet moss was slippery. Frankie sensed it happening and he reached for her hand, but it was too late. She lost her balance and fell.

Angel almost disappeared, all but her little hand sticking up out of the water. Frankie was sure he heard her call his name, although his ears were full of panic, the sound of his own heart beating hard and fast.

She was moving quickly down the river. Frankie scrambled off the log and, with a strength he didn't know he had, broke a green branch from a nearby tree. He ran as hard as he could through the alder wood to a shallow part of the river. The branch was light in his hands.

Angel was trying to swim. He saw her head

and her hands and he held the long stick out to her.

"Grab it," he pleaded. "Please."

Later, they said it was a miracle. She held on tight and he pulled her in. He pulled so hard his arms were stiff the next day and he couldn't move them.

"Oh Angel," he whispered as he dragged her out of the water and lay down beside her, covering her with his coat and trying to keep her warm with his own body.

"Don't tell mum."

12

In the Bighouse

Frankie was in the bighouse sitting on one of the top benches, where the smoke from the three big fires on the dirt floor was actually worst. His eyes hurt and he didn't even try to stop the tears that poured out of them. Normally, he would have wiped them away or moved closer to the fire where his family was sitting. It wasn't so bad on his eyes on the lowest level of benches where the dancers and their families sat.

The smoke rose up to the top bleachers, where guests were put a little distance from the business, and kids, who couldn't sit still through the hours of dancing and speeches, ran up and down, playing tag and amusing themselves until they finally fell asleep, wrapped in a blanket, their arms full of shiny quarters and apples and oranges given away during the ceremonies.

He wanted to be alone, as far away from the comfort of his mum and dad and aunts and uncles as he could. He chose the darkest farthest corner, where no one would notice he was lost in his thoughts.

There was so much going on in his head, he felt like a movie projector playing in reverse, the pictures all speeded up. It made him feel crazy most of the time, the worry about Mr. Smith and what might happen to the kids when it all got itself discovered somehow. It was his fault. He shouldn't have given in to Odie. Odie could be so persuasive and it made Frankie feel wonderful to be helping out. Also, he had to admit, he truly hated Mr. Smith, who knew how to make every kid in the class feel bad about themselves, even Melanie.

When Mr. Smith came to his house to talk to his mother about the day he played hookey, Frankie heard him say words like "Indians" and "irresponsible". That was when he felt himself fill up with this horrible bitter feeling. He wanted to run into the kitchen, where his mother and the teacher were having tea, and cover her ears.

She was proud of being a First Nations Person, and so was Frankie. There was nothing more wonderful to him than the music and dancing of his people and the art and the love in their families. He didn't want her to hear this stuff and he was sorry he made it happen, just because he thought it was a nice idea to take the afternoon off school and go see the salmon spawn, which was a very beautiful thing, much better than sitting in a stuffy classroom with the windows all shut taking sentences apart and smelling people's peanut butter and banana sandwiches rot in the garbage cans.

The other thing that worried him was using his special gift for the wrong things. He knew it was bad to be selfish with his powers, that they had come down through his family of chiefs and shamen to be used wisely, to help others and cure sickness, not just for tricks and jokes. That was why he never did things like wishing for ice-cream and new bicycles.

It was quieter in the bighouse. The drums were quiet and the dancing and singing had stopped for a while. They were doing the business. His father and uncles and the others were speaking their language and handing out dishes, blankets, money and fruit to the guests who had come to his cousin's naming dance.

Some of the visitors were going back and forth to the kitchen, getting cups of tea and bannock bread. Earlier in the evening, they had a big dinner of seal meat, salmon, and deer with potatoes. Everyone took turns eating with their families, but not Frankie. He hadn't eaten for three days and he wasn't going to until Mr. Smith turned up. He had decided. His mind and his stomach had to be calm. When he was past being hungry and the pictures in his brain focused so he could read them clearly, then maybe he could understand what he had to do next.

Over the noise of the crackling fire and pleasant murmur of chatting friends and relatives, he could hear the sound of his stomach begging for food. It didn't matter. Something strange was happening to him, like his magic trips, a kind of buzzing in his arms and legs that made him feel dead and alive at the same time, numb and yet strangely sensitive to every sound and touch. His head was beginning to separate from his body, which seemed to be filling itself with warmth and voices from another place. It wasn't scary. He knew from his zapper trips that he wouldn't feel any pain when the spirit came on him.

Soon he felt lighter than air, like a balloon rising, full of its own strange music. His eyes felt better. His stomach felt better. He wanted to laugh, but the noise that came out of his mouth, sounding to him like an echo from another world, was the cry of a bird.

It came over and over and he did nothing to stop it.

Frankie was lifted up and he didn't feel a thing. Hands, lots of them, the soft, kind hands of his uncles and cousins, carried him down past rows of relatives and friends to the floor, where they stood in a circle around him.

The drums had started up again. As they grew louder and louder, and the singing too, Frankie felt his hands and feet begin to move. He wasn't a chubby boy or a slow runner any more. He was a bird moving swiftly and gracefully around the fire. And he was singing. Everyone knew his song. The drums and rattles kept time as the singers chanted his grandfather's song. They knew it, just as he did. His aunties guided him round the fire.

The bighouse filled with the sound of his spirit coming out of a hundred mouths at once. It was as if his heart filled his whole body and made itself sound like a single drum in the home of his ancestors. Frankie had never known such joy.

Eventually, his head and body came together, and he felt himself empty of the feeling of becoming something else. The spirit rose from him, as if it were the weight of gentle hands on his shoulders.

He looked up, past the fire, past the smoke to the hole in the roof of the bighouse. Past all that, there was night and stars as bright and clear as fish in a spawning stream.

He watched that darkness become a blue and yellow light that shone on his face and made him blink. The drums stopped. The singing stopped. His feet stopped dancing. There was something like sunlight in the hole in the roof of the bighouse, and in the centre of the light was a blue and yellow bird.

13

Odie Has a Cold and Hears the News

"We did it!" Frankie practically yelled into the phone. "Ms. Take tried to strangle Bobby Roaf and his parents are suing the school. Mr. Willis sent her home, and she was blubbering like a baby baboon when she left. Oh," he sighed as if confronting a pair of peanut butter parfaits at the Dairy Queen two-for-one-sale with a large spoon, "it was beautiful. All this black stuff came out of her eyes and ran down her face. Somebody said it was acid rain and even Mr. Willis laughed. I saw him."

"Whad'd Bobby do?" Odie had a terrible cold. He'd got soaked rolling in the snow, with Jen on top of him like an Amazonian warrior the day of the bird search.

"Oh, nothing," Frankie said. "He was singing in quiet-reading time and she told him to stop, but he didn't. He was making this sound but his lips weren't moving. She couldn't prove it was him. She stood right over him and listened, but he still didn't stop. It was so funny. Everybody was laughing their heads off, which made her even madder. Then she started to make horrible noises like an old car starting up and she looked like she was going to explode. Pchheew." He made a kind of bursting noise, like the world's biggest pimple hitting the bathroom mirror.

"The next thing we knew, she had her hands around Bobby's neck and he couldn't breathe. She was right off her head. It was beautiful.

"All the kids got out of their seats and jumped on her. There was a huge dogpile and everyone was kicking and screaming. Mr. Willis heard us in the office and he came down. He didn't even get mad at us, just told her to go home and then she started whining and whimpering and there was stuff coming out of her nose too." Frankie thought for a minute. He wanted to paint it as lurid as possible.

"Did you know she had a bald spot?"

"Do I didn."

"Her wig came off. That's when she really started hooting and hollering. You should have seen Bobby's face. It was the colour of blackberry juice. She could of killed him."

"Baybe she should'b." Odie didn't like Bobby that much. He was a bragger and a bully. Odie had never heard him singing before, even in music class. He had some suspicion about who had really made the noise that got Bobby in trouble. "Den she'd hab to go to the 'lectric chair." He started to laugh and got into a fit of coughing.

"You shouldn't have let Jen push you in the snow," Frankie remarked.

"Who told you?"

"A little bird." It was Frankie's turn to laugh.

"Oh, cubbon. You habn been talking to birds hab you?" Odie's heart was beating so hard, he could feel it throbbing in his fingertips.

"There's one on my shoulder right now, and he's got terrible breath."

Odie yelled so loud, Frankie's eardrum just about popped, and he dropped the receiver.

"Dumb," said Mr. Smith into the mouthpiece. "Bad Boy!"

"It's hib. It's really hib. Where was he?" Oh how could he have got himself sick and missed the best day of school ever?

Actually, he'd been enjoying his cold, stretching it out as long as he could, having chicken soup, ice cream and ginger ale on trays, feeling his mother's cool hand on his forehead, waiting for his dad to come home at night with a comic book or a game or a model to glue together.

Being sick was a great luxury. It sure beat school, especially with substitute teachers these days being almost as bad as Mr. Smith.

Odie had been avoiding his responsibilities as Class President and instigator of The Disappearance. He was feeling a little guilty about it and he knew missing the excitement was his punishment.

Frankie waited, enjoying the torture of suspense. "Well?" Odie's voice rose up, almost to the high C he could reportedly sing, although that was a talent he downplayed at school for obvious reasons. "Where was he?"

"He came back." Frankie said flatly. "The window was open and he flew in."

"Didde say where he'd beed?" Odie asked, hopefully.

"Yeah. He had a little suitcase with him. It had stickers all over it. Peru, China, Timbuktu."

"Cbbon, Frankie. Was there a clue?"

Frankie hesitated. Some things were private, even among best friends.

"I saw him in a vision at the bighouse, when I was dancing. It was the first time. I never got the spirit before. Kids our age don't usually. It doesn't happen until you've been initiated, spent the winter in the bighouse away from your family, eating Indian food and going in the river every day to make yourself clean and ready for the spirit.

"Usually they grab you and take you there. You have to listen to the Elders and learn all the rules and also learn your song and your dance.

"I don't know why it happened to me like that. I was real hungry and had a lot of feelings. My head got all funny and then I sort of started singing and my uncles carried me down to the floor and I started dancing. It felt so good. I was moving like a bird and I was a bird. You can't believe it until it happens to you. The only words I knew were my song and it just came out of me without thinking about it. That was weird.

"And then it got quiet and it was all over. The feeling left me and all the singers and drummers stopped too, as if they knew the very moment it happened."

Frankie's voice got more excited. "There was this light coming through the smoke-hole in the roof. When I looked up, there he was in this incredible brightness, the most far-out thing you ever saw.

"And then the lights went out and he was gone and I didn't see him again until I got to school on Monday."

"Where d'ya think he was all dat tib?"

Frankie thought for a minute and took in a big breath. "I think he was inside me."

"Why?"

"Because of the way I was feeling and I know he was scared of Pusscat and Ms. Take and all the things that were happening."

"Why'd he cub back den?"

"I dunno. Maybe it got like jail and he wanted out again." Frankie shrugged, even though Odie couldn't see him. How could he understand all this stuff? It made him so tired just having it happen all alone, trying to figure it out and explain everything to his friend.

"Wha'd it feel like, really, when he cabe out."

"Like I blew my nose. How can I tell you, Odie? It makes me scared sometimes. I don't like to think about it too much. What if something really terrible happened and I got taken over by some monster like King Kong? What if I did something bad and hurt people? It's awful."

Odie was filled with sadness for his friend. It was like carrying the heaviest pack of all on a three-day camping trip. "You won't Frankie. You're a good person and you help peeble."

"Well, I need help now. We've got to figure out what to do next. You're the brains of this operation, Odie."

14

What to do with Mr. Smith

"I dunno, Frankie. He's acting different." As soon as Odie's cold was better, he got on his bike and hightailed it over to Frankie's place on the Stony Beach Reserve. The parrot flew to Odie's shoulder, contentedly cleaning his feathers, some of which were missing, thanks to Pusscat. From time to time, Odie felt something on his cheek that, if it hadn't been delivered by a beak, would have been a kiss. "Mr. Smith was never this nice."

Mr. Willis was taking grade six himself these days and he had outlawed birds from the classroom. "Too damn much trouble and confusion." Besides, the killer cat was ubiquitous and nobody wanted slaughter in the schools. Mice yes, but not birds. People got attached to birds, got to know them by name. It wouldn't do Mr. Willis any good to have that sort of thing going on at Tzouhalem Elementary. He had his reputation to think of, and his pension. The parrot could not stay.

That suited Frankie fine. He took the bird and his bag of seed home that very first day, when he mysteriously reappeared. People stopped their cars to watch him riding along on his bicycle with Mr. Smith perched on his handlebars, making happy noises, with the wind in his face.

The Zapper family took to the bird. They didn't have a cat and the sisters were happy to clean up the seed he spat everywhere. They liked talking to him. "Pretty girls," he said over and over as they laughed and blushed.

Frankie was sitting on the edge of his bed, making zaps, when Odie came into his room. Some of them had been falling off the ceiling and, besides, he needed to make new paths for better trips. The old ones were interfering too much with his real life. He wanted to go someplace where school and birds were just words in a foreign language.

"I agree with you," he said wearily, swirling a ball of paper and goober in his cheek and spitting it out on the silver foil. "I think it must have had something to do with my dance. I think I was possessed by the spirit of the bird just as the bird was possessed by Mr. Smith. When I became me again, maybe the same thing happened with the parrot. Probably Mr. Smith has left him and gone someplace else." He shrugged his shoulders. "Don't ask me. It's so complicated." Frankie was sick of complications. He wanted his life to be as clear as the river when it hadn't rained for a long time. He just wanted to float along and let his dreams speak. This

Mr. Smith business got everybody mad and mixed up and was likely to get them into trouble bigger than the person who dreamed up The Black Book ever even thought of.

The last thing Frankie wanted was to end up in some jail for kids like the school Odie's parents were threatening to send him to. He didn't want to have to eat honky food, or wear a uniform, or run in the rain, or get up and go to sleep at the same time every day. He'd rather die.

"I'd rather die," he said out loud.

"What?" Odie jerked out of his own thoughts.

"Oh nothing. I was thinking about that stupid school you're going to."

"I won't go. I'll run away."

"Oh, sure, and do what?" Odie tried to act big, but Frankie knew perfectly well the bodybuilder waited on him hand and foot. Odie could hardly tie his own shoelaces.

"Who's going to blow your nose for you?"

"Very funny, Frankie. You should try being an only child. It's a big pain in the elbow. Every time you get the flu, they think you're going to die. A "B" on your report card means you're going to be a failure in life, instead of a doctor or a lawyer. You're not allowed to get dirty. You're not allowed to get cavities. The best thing that ever happened to me was when my mother discovered her fat. Now she's got something else to think about."

"She looks okay," Frankie said appreciatively. He was starting to notice girls.

"She's no Marilyn Monroe," Odie remarked, "and, to tell you the truth, it's embarrassing walking around with a thirty-eight-year-old woman in pink plastic pants. My mother looks like a rainbow that went through a food processor."

"Is she that old?" Frankie ignored the comments about Odie's mother's clothes because he thought they were nice. He liked bright colours. "I can't believe anyone could be that old."

"How old d'you think Mr. Smith is?" Odie asked, pushing his glasses back up his nose.

"He must be at least thirty something. His brain's gone completely."

"If Mr. Smith has left Mr. Smith," Odie said stroking the calm and affectionate pet that had replaced their irritable parrot, " I wonder where he is?"

15

The Plot Thickens

On Monday morning, it sounded like the dentists were having a convention outside the 6A classroom. Odie could hear buzzing and squealing from the bottom of the stairs, where he and Frankie were waiting until the last possible moment to rush up the stairs and into their seats before the final bell.

The parrot was cosily hidden away under Frankie's Cowichan sweater, with a branch of millet to keep him quiet. They had decided to bring him to school and risk the wrath of Mr. Willis, because, as Odie said, he was probably the only one who knew the whereabouts of the spirit or substance of their missing teacher. By now, they had agreed that the bird had most definitely separated himself and was just a parrot with a big mouth again, not the transformed presence of an adult nerd.

"GO GO GO!" the former Mr. Smith repeated, as Frankie attempted to find his face under the sweater and muzzle it. That wily bird knew he

6A

was in cat territory. He was smart enough to know Mr. Willis' feline sidekick wouldn't give up until she had the rest of the feathers and a little meat for her sandwich too.

"Shut-up. I won't let her get you." They were running up the stairs now, Frankie puffing a little and hoping the bird didn't show.

All the kids were still in the hall. The atmosphere was hysterical. Frankie almost forgot the bulge in his chest. Jen saw them first and fought her way through the knot of terrified kids. "He's back!" she said in a loud whisper, as the others quieted down and made a path, so Frankie and Odie could take a close look at the situation.

With the kind of heart in your throat feeling you have when you look at the sun during an eclipse or walk into traffic blindfolded, Frankie and Odie, last-chance gamblers, risked their skins and took a look through the smoky glass window in the classroom door.

They stood for a moment, listening to the blood pounding in their ears. It was the sound of absolute terror, waves crashing on a stormy beach. The parrot was still in Frankie's breast.

"It's him alright," Odie said, finally, screwing his eyes up tight. "I'd know that suit anywhere."

"What'll we do?" Melanie started to cry. "You got us into this."

"Plug her," Odie ordered, and Jen put her

rolled-up fist in Melanie's mouth, which was a brave thing to do because Melanie's teeth were sharp and her bands dangerous.

"Go in and act normal," he said. "We don't know anything, remember." He opened the door and the kids slowly and quietly filed in and took their seats.

Mr. Smith was sitting on his desk, knees crossed, one leg swinging, his blue pantleg torn, showing several inches of skinny, hairy leg. His arms were crossed too. He had a nasty smile stuck on the bottom half of his face.

He waited until they all sat down, then stood up, grabbed his big blackboard ruler and smashed it down on the desk, breaking it in half, an exercise they all remembered and feared as the prelude to further displays of childish temper.

"You nasty little brats have really cooked yourselves this time." Odie could feel the room spinning and shaking, as thirty sets of bones and teeth rattled.

"I don't know exactly what happened here, but..." He looked directly at Melanie, who was blubbering silently, "I intend to find out."

He paused to look around the room, taking possession of every fearful heart with his malevolent stare. It took ages. Maybe a minute or two. Some of them felt like throwing up.

"Two days ago, I was discovered sitting in a

tree," Jen gave Odie her I TOLD YOU SO look. Where else would you expect to find a fruitcake like Mr. Smith? She knew it all along. "... in Ladysmith, sixty miles from here. A policeman was fetched to get me down and I bit him, for which crime I was placed under arrest." He held up one very unattractive leg and said accusingly. "My pants were torn. My only suit is ruined. Somebody will have to pay."

He began to pace and smack his left fist into the palm of his right hand. "It is coming back to me slowly." He looked around the room, enjoying the panic written on every face. They all knew they were cooked.

"My family was frantic. I almost lost my job." He gave them a look of purest hatred, "I know this class, the worst, most undisciplined class I have ever taught, is responsible for my suffering. And," his voice rose like a whining tornado, pulling them all out of their desks up into the air, "I will get revenge if it's the last thing I ever do. I will have blood."

"Bad boy. Bad boy," the parrot poked his head out between Frankie's buttons and shrieked at Mr. Smith, who lit up like a juke box gone berserk and leapt on Frankie, screaming incoherently, "You mongrel twit! I'll fix you!" He grabbed his former namesake by one leg and held him high over his head. "I know what I'll do. I'll make this wretched bird into parrot soup, and you can jolly well drink it or serve ten years of detentions."

Before anyone could think that they'd all be gone in ten years anyway, out in the real world where Mr. Smith would be only a horrible memory, he was gone, right out of the classroom, with his squawking victim tightly grasped.

The kids, scared paralytic, sat with their mouths open for several seconds as the door banged shut and Mr. Smith went cursing down the hall, bumping into lockers negligently left open.

"After him!" somebody shouted, and they were off like a shot, all thirty of them. Nobody was sick or pretending to be sick. They were all there for the last battle.

16

Everyone Gets What They Deserve

Mr. Smith ran down the stairs, out the door and headed for the parking lot, limping as if his torn pantleg was an actual wound. When his old wreck of a car refused to start, he got out and kicked it, bruising his foot. He was still holding his hostage by one scrawny leg.

Mr. Smith was cursing, the bird was squawking and the kids banged on the trunk and yelled, as the car coughed alive and lurched slowly out of the schoolground.

"Run!" Jen yelled, her long legs taking several yards in every stride. "Get your bikes. Follow that man. Don't let him out of your sight!"

It was over a mile to the tacky bungalow, where Mr. and Mrs. Smith and their unfortunate daughter lived in wretchedness together. The place was stuck on a square of dull grass, without a single flower or shrub to brighten it up.

That was where he was heading, stopping and starting and jerking away from stopsigns. It was clear the parrot was making it almost impossible for him to steer the car, let alone change gears. Riding piggy back was a blur of a boy in red glasses.

The street was full of kids, kids on bikes, kids in slippers and stocking feet. Stragglers, late for school, joined the fast parade tailing Mr. Smith and his rust-coloured wreck. Odie, sliding between the roof and the trunk, was holding on for dear life.

The town went crazy. Someone rang the fire alarm. Somebody else ran to get the photographer from the newspaper. Witnesses selling copies of The Watchtower outside the post office dropped the papers and ran. Customers left their morning coffee at

the Cedar and went to see what the commotion was about. People in cars were honking their horns. They thought it must be a special day and the town was out to celebrate.

Mr. Smith lurched to a stop in front of his house. Odie dropped to the pavement and ran after him, but not fast enough. The front door slammed in his face, and he heard it lock. A passerby looked in the window and saw Mrs. Smith throw all 250 pounds of herself against the door as her husband ran to the kitchen and rummaged frantically, looking for a big enough pot to make a really royal pot of soup. He was laughing like a lunatic, a sound that escaped to the out-of-doors where kids and townspeople were gathering.

That noise made the hair stand up on their spines. They knew something radical had to be done, and fast. When Frankie arrived, all short of breath, he wanted to climb on the roof and go down the chimney, but he got caught halfway up on the drainpipe and was hanging there, calling to Odie, who paid no attention.

Jen yelled again. "Somebody call the cops! Get the S.P.C.A!" Just then, a firetruck rolled up, its siren wailing, and several confused volunteer firemen, who had just fallen out of their beds or come off a night shift, sniffed around for signs of smoke.

Odie was looking around for a rock to break the living room window, but SuperJen couldn't wait another minisecond. In a minute or two, the soup would be on.

She ran back to the street, looked straight at the front door, took a deep breath and ran up the walk, up the stairs and straight into two inches of solid wood and a ton of Mrs. Smith. The door crashed in, Mrs. Smith rolled backwards, and Jen entered triumphant over the mess on the mat, pressed on by the cheers of hundreds of kids and neighbours and sleepy firemen. She raced to the kitchen and saw the homicidal Mr. Smith lifting the lid off the pot.

Just in time, she took a super leap and knocked him off his pins. As he fell, he let out a blood-curdling scream. The smell of his breath nearly knocked her out, but she held on.

The parrot, released from his terrible grip, shrieked and flew out the front door, straight to Frankie, who had been brought down at last with the help of a ladder from the firetruck.

It didn't take long for the police and the S.P.C.A. to arrive. They wrote down thirty different versions of the story, had a conference in the garage, and decided to arrest Mr. Smith, who was taken to the police car in handcuffs.

Mr. Willis, who had been in his office doing target practice with a water pistol he had confiscated the previous Friday, had hitched a ride with the police chief, who came by way of the school. He stood on the front porch and raised his hand for silence.

"Mr. Smith is fired," he said to the loudest cheer of the day. "And there will be a holiday today for grade six. But first, we will all go to the Cedar Cafe for milkshakes, and it's on me." He reminded himself to take the money out of Mr. Smith's severance pay.

Rumours spread like brushfire in the town, as Jen was carried shoulder high through the streets to the restaurant. Nobody knew for sure exactly what happened, but they knew a black cloud had been lifted off their community. Some grown-ups remembered the torture they suffered when Mr. Smith was their teacher, and they formed a committee to suggest that the government should design a special postage stamp to commemorate this day, with Jen on it, of course, and the parrot, and maybe even Odie and Frankie if they could all fit in.

Jen was in heaven when her dad phoned a few days later to say he had read about her in the newspaper. "That's my girl," he said, and she felt goosepimples all over. Her dad sounded lonely. Secretly, she made plans to get her parents back together at Christmas time. They would kiss under the mistletoe.

Odie's parents made his reprieve official. They lived in a good town full of good kids, and they were not going to send their only child off to boarding school. This was lucky for Odie and for the guys at school. He was about to receive some very good mail as a result of sending letters of complaint to candy companies about their products. Soon, he had been told in apologetic answers to his criticism of stale and underweight treats, he would be receiving boxes of their confections by parcel post. There would be enough chocolate bars to give a lifetime of cavities to the whole class.

Frankie Zapper gratefully accepted all the chocolates and cookies showered on him when he was dude of the day. He took them home and shared them with his sisters and the sweet-toothed parrot who snored at the end of his bed from that day until this, because parrots live almost forever.

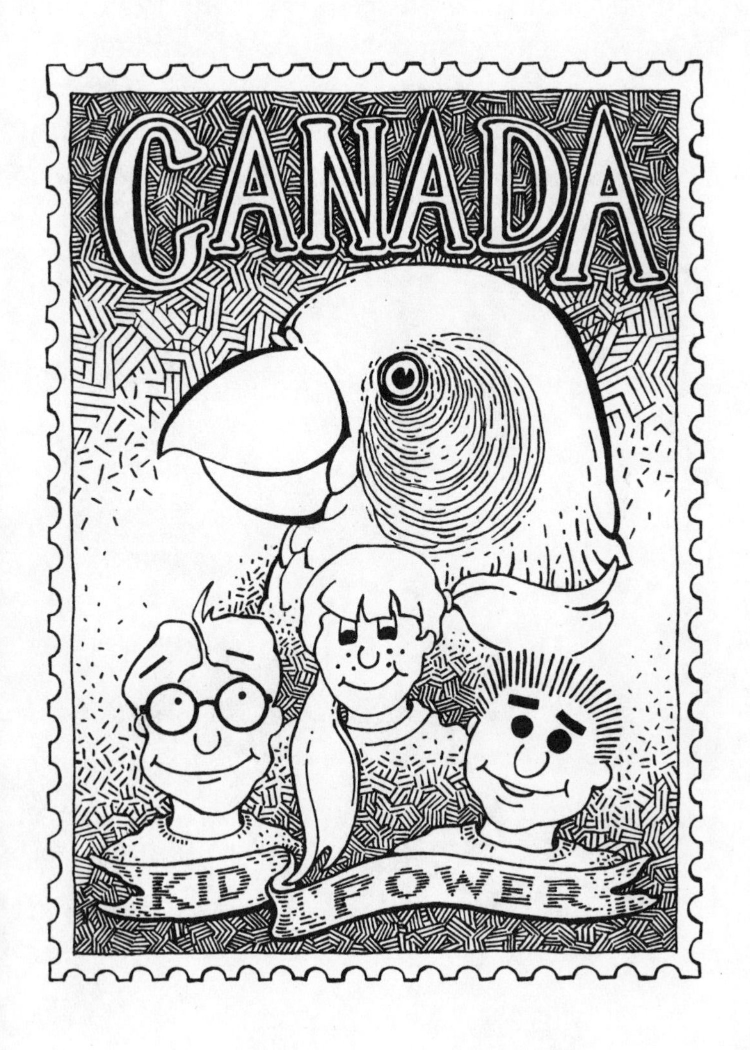
CANADA
KID POWER

ABOUT THE AUTHOR AND ILLUSTRATOR

This story was written by Linda Rogers, with help from her son Tristan, who is a lot like Odie. She writes books for people of all ages and, with her husband Rick, writes songs for kids.

Rick Van Krugel is a blues musician and illustrator. You can tell from his pictures that he is a funny guy who knows it is sometimes hard to be a kid. Rick and Linda perform together at schools and festivals.